"How close are you **undercover assignment?" Kayla asked.**

"We're weeks away from making an arrest. I'm only missing the last piece of the puzzle, and I can put this whole thing to bed."

Kayla blew out a breath. "Conner, this is huge."

"And I don't want you getting caught in the middle of it. I don't know what Andis wants with you. All I know is that it won't be good. I'll protect you if I can, but if you even suspect you're in danger you call the sheriff. Understand?"

Kayla nodded. "Of course. I just...wish there was a way to help."

Conner took two steps toward her. "I don't want you anywhere near Andis."

Being here with her, knowing that Kayla knew the truth of the man he'd been pretending to be for months, Conner felt right for the first time since... he didn't know. Maybe since that night ten years ago when Kayla had been in trouble and he'd saved her from what that man had planned.

He wouldn't leave her side until he knew she was safe.

Lisa Phillips is a British-born, tea-drinking, guitar-playing wife and mom of two. She and her husband lead worship together at their local church. Lisa pens high-stakes stories of mayhem and disaster where you can find made-for-each-other love that always ends in a happily-ever-after. She understands that faith is a work in progress more exciting than any story she can dream up. Lisa blogs monthly at teamloveontherun.com, and you can find out more about her books at authorlisaphillips.com.

Books by Lisa Phillips

Love Inspired Suspense

Secret Service Agents

Security Detail

Double Agent
Star Witness
Manhunt
Easy Prey
Sudden Recall
Dead End

SECURITY DETAIL

LISA PHILLIPS

HARLEQUIN® LOVE INSPIRED® SUSPENSE

Recycling programs
for this product may
not exist in your area.

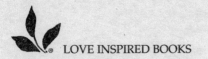 LOVE INSPIRED BOOKS

ISBN-13: 978-0-373-67813-6

Security Detail

Copyright © 2017 by Lisa Phillips

www.Harlequin.com

Printed in U.S.A.

Though an army encamp against me, my heart shall not fear; though war arise against me, yet I will be confident.
—Psalms 27:3

I'm so thankful to God for inspiring me with another idea for a series. I hope you all enjoy reading them as much as I'll enjoy writing these Secret Service books!

ONE

Kayla Harris shoved the key in the lock of her office door and glanced one more time down the dark hallway. Streetlights lit a swatch of the wood floor through the window at the end of the hall. Cold fingered the back of her neck, a sensation that hadn't let up all day. Not since that weird phone call this afternoon. It was probably all in her head that she'd been able to hear someone breathing on the other end.

Why did she have to forget that file? She should be home. Safe.

For eight years she hadn't had a Secret Service detail to watch out for her, and not once had she thought she might need it—until right now. What was different tonight? The fear was probably all her imagination.

Kayla sighed, mostly at her overactive imagination, and turned the key. The door swung open before she could unlock it. She didn't move, just stood in the hall and looked inside.

Footsteps. Heavy shoes on the wood of the stairs ascended to the second floor above the Main Street bakery in Samson, Virginia. The only entrance and exit for the second floor. The rental space was at the north end of Main. Quaint town, nice people who had the decency to—for the most part—not mention the things she'd done as a young adult.

Since she'd lived in the White House at the time, it meant that everyone in the country knew her story. A mother who had passed away from cancer, her father just reelected for his second term. Kayla had…gone off the rails, to put it pleasantly. But that was years ago, and she didn't need to be reminded of the White House or those days so soon after her mother had passed.

It wasn't hiding, living the small-town life. Not if everyone knew who she was. She'd spent her teen years tormenting the White House staff, the Secret Service—particularly the agents assigned to her—and her father with her wild ways. But that was years ago. Now she liked her quiet life of prenuptial agreements, wills and contracts. Most of which involved her sitting at her desk and not in a courtroom. Sure, it was an illusion of anonymity, but it was her life and she liked it.

And now this.

Someone was coming, and there was no time to run to the fire exit.

Kayla ducked inside and gripped the handle so it made no sound when she closed and locked the door. She pulled out her phone, clicked on the flashlight and shone it around. The fact that her office had been torn apart didn't register. It couldn't; there was no time.

Kayla wasn't alone. That was all she needed to know.

She dialed 911. The operator answered, an older lady she'd met at church who said everything like it was and didn't mince words. Her phone chimed. *Low battery.* Kayla opened her mouth to reply to the operator and heard those heavy steps in the hallway. The reply choked in her throat. *Help.*

Her office had been searched. Destroyed. Had they waited around for her?

Kayla's heart pounded in her chest until she thought it might burst. She raced to the far side of her "lawyer desk," the one her father had bought her after she had passed the Virginia bar. Her father, former president Jefferson Harris, would send a batch of Secret Service agents to protect her if she asked him to. But it would be too late.

Kayla crouched and hugged her jacket tight to her chest with her purse in her lap. *Lord.* She was a whole different person now than she'd been all those years ago, a "new creation," God called her. She had peace with God. She needed some of that peace now.

A floorboard in the hall creaked.

She looked around for something to defend herself with, spotted an umbrella in the corner where she hung her coat and rushed to grab it. She couldn't hide; she had to fight. Brandishing the thing like a weapon, Kayla waited as the sound of her own breath rushed through her ears.

The door handle twisted.

"Hey!" A man's voice. But not from the other side of the door. This was farther away. The handle was released and the heavy steps pounded down the hall. A second set followed, giving chase to the far end. *Bang. Bang.* Glass shattered. Kayla dropped her purse on the floor and covered her ears as she stepped back until her shoulders hit the wall.

"Stop!" A man's voice.

Then all she could hear was the thump of her heart in her chest. She lowered her hands. What was happening? Should she run? Call 911 again? Scream for help? Her phone lay on the floor by the desk, the screen lit but too far away for her to see if the call was still active.

Again, cold fingered the back of her neck. All

too reminiscent of the night she'd snuck into a club so many years ago and had been slipped something in her drink. If Conner hadn't found her, who knew what might have happened that night. But Special Agent Conner Thorne hadn't thought his actions anything special. *Just doing my job, Ms. Harris.* She'd rolled her eyes, but inside, she'd been about to cry at the fact that he could be so impersonal with her. Especially when the feelings she'd had for the twenty-six-year-old Secret Service agent were anything but. Like a four-year age difference really made him "too old for her."

Conner had been her first real crush. Her first real sense of what love might be. She'd never met anyone in college who brought out those feelings. Then he'd come along that last year her father was in the White House and she'd never met anyone else since who measured up.

More recently, Kayla had heard he'd been fired from the Secret Service. Something else she'd put behind her to add to the list of things she'd moved on from.

Still, thinking of him gave her peace. *Thank You, Lord.*

A shadow darkened the office doorway. The door was cracked only a few inches, but she saw it. The person pushed open the door slowly, hesitantly. A killer on the prowl? Kayla wanted to run to her phone, but was it worth the risk when the move might cost her her life?

After a deep breath, Kayla called out, "If you take one step in here, I'll blow your head off!"

"You don't like guns."

That voice.

The light flipped on.

That face.

Kayla dropped the umbrella.

The lips on his scruffy face curled up at the corners. "Were you planning on skewering me with that thing? I'm having a bad enough day already."

Kayla pressed one hand to her throat. "You scared me half to death with that cloak-and-dagger entrance, Conner Thorne."

"Ah, so you haven't forgotten me." His lips broke into a smile. Conner Thorne. He still gave off that air of boyish charm, but there was nothing boyish about this man. Dark jeans, heavy boots, a button-up shirt and a leather jacket. His chocolate-brown hair needed cutting, and he badly needed to shave.

"You look like a thug."

"And you look like a lawyer." He stepped into the room and closed the door behind him. "Though I guess that's the point in both cases."

"What are you doing here?" This was so weird. "Do you…live here in town or something?"

"Or something." Conner glanced around the room. "Nice place. Nice town, too. I've been here and around for almost six months now."

"Six—" She choked. "And you're just coming to say hi *now*?"

He smiled again. "Not exactly."

"Was that you in the hall?"

"I shot wide and chased him off. He ran down the fire escape at that end. But he saw my face."

That seemed to be a bad thing, as Conner's brow furrowed over his blue eyes.

"Who was it?"

He looked around her office like he was trying to figure out a puzzle. "Did you make this mess?"

Kayla exhaled and crossed the room. "Yeah, I just love cleaning so much I make messes on purpose." She swiped up the phone. The call to 911 had disconnected. Did that mean Sheriff Johnson was on his way? "I figured whoever that was, he did this after I left work. I was picking up a file I'd forgotten that I need to work on this weekend." She laid a hand on her roiling stomach and tried to take a deep breath. "He must have done this, then come back. Maybe he followed me. Who was it?"

"Someone I...work with."

So he was a thug, for real? Kayla had heard he got fired after he was discredited. Too many indiscretions committed and too few orders followed. He'd never been one to toe the line, but she never dreamed he'd go this far.

Kayla glanced at the window, suddenly feeling less safe with this man who'd once been a friend.

How long until the police arrived?

The sheriff was a friend, a nice older man who protected this county fiercely. Sheriff Johnson referred battered women to her when they wanted to get help but didn't know where to go. She'd done some good in this county that had nothing to do with her job and everything to do with a desire that no woman should ever feel the way she'd felt that night years ago. A victim.

The fear sat in her middle, unfurling like a snake ready to strike at her again.

Conner studied the room, then glanced at her. "When the sheriff gets here, tell him everything." He checked his watch. "I don't want to read about your grisly demise in the paper while I'm drinking my morning coffee. Okay?"

Kayla folded her arms. He couldn't have known that man had tossed her office, couldn't have faked that surprise. He knew that he didn't need to do that with her when they'd always been honest with each other, even when it was hard. So why had he shown up tonight? "One condition."

"What's that?" He shifted his stance. Was he really so eager to leave her?

"Tell me why you're here."

Conner ignored the question. Being in the same room as President Harris's daughter again was messing with his head. The cute young woman had grown into a strikingly beautiful lady who looked nothing like the Ivy League princess he'd imagined she would eventually become. She'd certainly straightened herself out from those days of pink streaks in her blond hair just to annoy her father and risky outfits her mother never would have approved of.

Conner couldn't say the same for himself. Not if he wanted to keep his story straight...and in line with what the world believed had become of him. His handler had agreed Conner should check on Kayla, but Greg had also told him that under no circumstances should he read Kayla in on his secret.

But that was before Pete had seen his face. No doubt he was here with Manny, the only one of Andis Bamir's men who actually had brains. But the boss couldn't have meant for them to break in and then try to grab Kayla. Could he?

Either way, Pete knew Conner was here. His cover was blown. He'd interfered with whatever they had planned, and they knew it. Manny was probably calling the boss right now. The order would go out, and Conner would have a target on his back.

He glanced at Kayla. He could slip out before the sheriff got here. They still had a minute to talk, and then she'd be safe again. "Tell me why someone wants to scare you. What do you have in here that they need?"

Kayla shrugged. "Why should I answer that when you don't want to answer my question?"

"No boyfriend? An admirer? Someone who asked you out but you turned them down?" It chafed to ask the question, but he had to know. Years ago a relationship with her would have been inappropriate and against protocol. Now it would put her in danger.

She pressed her lips together. "Not that it's any of your business, but I am not interested in men who only want to talk about how wild I was. That's not me anymore, but for some reason they only want to see if that girl's still in there. Well, no more. I'd like to meet someone who doesn't know who I am and isn't going to judge me based on the past."

"Kayla, everyone knows who you are."

"Hence the reason why there's no one in my life, past or present." She shook her head. "I haven't done anything."

"That likely isn't the case. You just don't know what it is yet."

"Why do you always have to be so literal? Not everything is cut-and-dried, Conner. If I knew who did this, then there wouldn't be a problem." Kayla pinned him with a look. Call him crazy, but he'd missed that look. She said, "You know who that was in the hall."

"The less you know, the better, Kayla. Let me take care of this on my end, and I'll do my best to keep you out of it." He was going to have to leave now. Walk away from her. Again. "Tell the sheriff everything you know. Do everything he says you should do to stay safe. Including calling the Secret Service."

It would be simpler if she got Secret Service help.

She tipped her head to one side, which usually spelled trouble. Or more paperwork. Which to a Secret Service agent was essentially the same thing. "And we've circled all the way back to my original question. Why. Are. You. Here?" She folded her arms. Also a bad sign. "Answer the question, Conner."

Okay, so she was a really good lawyer. Kayla had won a few national debates in college. He hadn't seen it but he believed it. He'd never found argumentative to be cute before, and he intended on enjoying it while he could. It would be over soon and he'd likely never see her again.

"I'm here to check on you. To make sure everything is okay." Which it wasn't, not now that he knew Andis Bamir wanted something from Kayla.

When she didn't say anything, he sighed. "I heard your name come up in conversation, okay? The people who were talking about you are bad people, and I knew it couldn't be good, so I came over to make sure you're okay. I don't know if they're planning something, but the fact that you've hit their radar is never good."

"Who are 'they'?"

"Andis Bamir. And his men."

Kayla's mouth opened. No sound came out. She shook her head. "Andis… Okay. Right. The nastiest man in three counties is talking about me, and we don't know why."

We. That was nice. Conner would jump at the chance to team up with her, but it wasn't possible. He checked his watch. The sheriff had better hurry. Though the delay gave him more time with Kayla.

She touched each finger in turn and paced her office. "Drug trafficking. Illegal arms sales. Counterfeit bills. Human—" She looked at him, and Conner nodded. "Of course he's doing every awful thing a person can do that involves breaking the law. Except that no one can catch him in the act or find any evidence."

"Because he spreads it around. Richmond. Washington. Norfolk. Everywhere is part of his 'territory' and he has a network of men all over the place."

Kayla stared at him. "How do you know the intricacies of his operation?"

"I can't tell you."

He saw in her eyes that her brain puzzled out the problem. "Money. Secret Service." Her mouth dropped open. "There was a rumor someone in town was printing counterfeit bills, but the sheriff couldn't figure out where it originated. It was only hearsay."

Conner waited.

"You're investigating it. The newspaper article said you'd been fired." Kayla lifted a finger to point at him, totally contrary to her upperclass upbringing. "You're undercover."

"I said I couldn't tell you, but since my cover is now blown wide open, I guess it doesn't hurt. I trust you to keep my secret, Kayla."

"You're working for Andis Bamir, trying to gather the evidence to put him away."

Conner wanted to hug her. "I can neither confirm nor deny that."

"Of course you can't." She started to pace back and forth. "It's an incredibly delicate and dangerous situation to be in." She wheeled around and stared at him. "Have you been undercover all this time, since the article?"

He nodded.

"That was years ago!"

"Assignments. More than one."

"How close are you to finishing this?"

"I'm only missing the last piece of the puzzle. Then I can put this whole thing to bed."

Andis Bamir's counterfeit bills had stopped flowing. The operation had halted for some reason, which meant any chance at catching him in the act had disappeared. He'd been ready to call it quits when he heard Kayla's name come up.

Kayla blew out a breath. "Conner, this is huge."

"And I don't want you getting caught in the middle of it. I don't know what Andis wants with you. All I know is that it can't be good. Tell the sheriff, and call your father. Get the Secret Service here to protect you. I don't want you to take any risks."

He could tell she didn't like that, but he wasn't going to give her the choice. Her safety was his top priority.

Conner took two steps toward her. "I don't want you anywhere near Andis."

Being here with her, knowing that Kayla knew the truth about the man he'd been pretending to be for months, Conner felt right for the first time since…he didn't know when. Maybe since that night years ago when Kayla had been in trouble and he'd saved her from what that man had planned.

But Conner couldn't be the person she'd known. Not here. No one could know that Conner. It was the nature of the job. Just the fact that Kayla knew the whole story made him feel like he was seeing the sun after a week of gray clouds.

"Wow." The word was a low mutter as she processed everything she'd learned and the implications.

Conner looked up. There was so much in her eyes he didn't know where to start. She cared about him; that was clear. He'd never met a more complicated woman, and he was about as straightforward as a man could be. It was probably good they'd never had the chance to be together. They'd likely have driven each other crazy.

He sighed. "I should le—"

The window smashed. A flaming bottle flew to the ground and burst open, spilling its contents across the floor.

Before the liquid could erupt into flames, Conner's Secret Service training kicked in and he dove toward Kayla.

TWO

Kayla hit the ground. Conner landed beside her as breath burst from her lungs. Flames erupted across the room and Kayla screamed. Conner pushed up off the floor and then grabbed her. She wobbled on her feet for a second and had time to grab her phone but not her laptop bag before he pulled her toward the door.

They made it to the hall, but he headed for the back of the building. No one else was there except them, not anyone from the dentist's office next to hers or the stores below. *Thank You, Lord.* There was no one else to get hurt, but there was also no one else who could call for help.

The men had come back, and now they were trying to kill them? What was going on?

Kayla raced after Conner. Halfway down the hall, another bottle came through the broken window at the far end. Conner shoved her to the wall and shielded her with his body. It was heroic, but it didn't mean he actually cared about her. Secret Service agents weren't paid for their feelings. They were paid to keep their charges from bodily harm. Still, she warmed at the care he was taking to make sure she wasn't exposed—to be certain danger reached him first.

"He's boxing us in. I've seen them do it before," Conner yelled over the crack and hiss of flames. "Is there another way out?"

"The dentist's office has a fire exit with stairs down to the ground floor."

Conner pointed down the hall. "On the side?" She nodded. "Too exposed. Anything else?"

Kayla glanced around, as though the answer would reveal itself through the walls. "We should call the sheriff again and find out where he is. Give me your phone—mine is almost dead."

He ran a hand through his hair and shook his head. "My cover is blown." He paused, his thoughts somewhere distant she wasn't invited. "I guess the rules no longer apply."

Kayla let her gaze roam his face, trying to figure out what on earth would possess a man to live the kind of life where he was constantly under threat of being killed.

She'd understood on some level before tonight that undercover work was dangerous for a law enforcement officer. But now that she'd seen what he lived with, Kayla didn't know if she could stand that life. There were men and women who could, though, and she had so much respect for what they did.

"So what do we do?"

Conner glanced around. "We need a place to hide where the smoke won't get us. We can call the sheriff from there. I just have to keep you safe until he shows up."

"But not yourself?" He didn't need to be safe?

"You know what I mean, Kayla. When I know you're okay, I'll make a break for it."

Instead of dishing it back to him—and dying of smoke inhalation from standing in this hallway—Kayla grabbed his arm and dragged him to the kitchen. Conner shut the door and she got two bottles of water from the fridge. Then he soaked some towels and tucked them under the door.

She handed him a water.

"Thanks." Conner drank half the bottle in one go and then pulled out his phone, thumbed buttons. After gulping down the rest of the water, he threw the empty bottle in the recycling bin.

Kayla looked around. "I think we should try to get out of here."

"They started the fire to flush you out, and now they're waiting outside. When you run outside, they'll probably shoot you. That's how this works. The fire gets you outside, and then they finish you off. If there's time, they'll dump the body back inside to destroy the evidence."

"Wonderful. Unless…"

"What?"

"They're trying to kill *you*. You said your cover is blown. Maybe they're not after me anymore." She saw the look he gave her and said, "Well, it's possible. And either way we need to get out of here before we suffocate." She grabbed his phone.

Conner's eyes darkened. "That isn't going to happen to you."

"Because I'm in danger, and you're going to save me?"

"Yes."

"You know, normal people just call the police when they're in danger." She even dialed the numbers to prove it.

Conner didn't react, though she knew for a fact she was funny. "You're not normal people and neither am I."

Kayla showed him the phone and pressed Dial. Just so he could see how normal she was. "I've been working very hard for the last few years to be normal, thank you, and you're ruining— Yes, I need the sheriff and a fire truck. I'm trapped in my office."

The same lady who'd answered the first time

took her location and Kayla answered a half-dozen questions. No, they weren't in danger of being immediately injured—though it would be minutes before their situation changed. No, they couldn't get out.

When the woman tried to get her to take deep breaths to calm down, she hung up. "Why did you come tonight?"

"Like I told you, I overheard a conversation from the next room. Your name was mentioned, so I decided to come over and see if you knew why they were talking about you. It's no secret that you or I once lived in the White House. That's probably why they didn't let me in on it."

"So you heard the conversation?"

"Not much of it, like I said. No more than your name, but I got the impression they don't like you too much."

"I don't know why not. I'm a likable person." Kayla wasn't like a trial lawyer who spent all day in a courtroom and made tons of enemies. She wrote wills. Business contracts. Nothing to hide. No one wanted her dead. That was crazy. Unless…

Conner frowned. "Something just happened with your face."

"I—" Kayla blew out a breath.

"Tell me."

"It can't be connected to me, so there's no

way they could know. But I own a piece of property on the outskirts of town. Sometimes the sheriff refers women in…dangerous situations to me. If they want to press charges against their husbands or boyfriends or whoever is hurting them, I can help them, but sometimes they're still in danger even then. So I give them a place to stay. Whether it's permanent or just until they get on their feet is up to them."

"You run a battered-women's shelter."

"Why did you say that like it's a bad thing?" Smoke had started to creep under the kitchen door. Kayla coughed. "I help women, and sometimes kids, too. But I don't run it—I have a manager for that. I just…facilitate the place. Locke helped me set it up."

"Of course Special Agent Locke helped you."

Okay, now he looked mad. What was it he'd said…? *Something just happened with your face.* Yeah, ditto. Didn't he like his former supervisor?

"Look," Kayla said. "I just thought if someone wanted to find something or hurt me, that would be the only reason I can think of as to why. Maybe they were looking for the address. The sheriff keeps a tight lid on the whole thing, but it could be that my identity was leaked and someone wants to get revenge on me for helping one of the women."

It wasn't like she could sit by and do nothing, though. Her job wasn't exactly on the front lines of making the world a better place, not like Mr. Undercover Agent over there. They couldn't all be like that. Kayla just used her passion to help women who needed it, and she gave them the chance to find safety. To feel real peace for the first time.

"So what's the connection between the shelter and Andis?"

Kayla shook her head. "You tell me."

"There has to be one." He glanced aside for a minute.

"Either way, we're both in a burning building." Kayla started toward the window to see if she could see a fire truck or at least emergency lights.

Conner grabbed her arm. "Don't go near the window. They might be watching for us."

Kayla was supposed to be done with the part of her life where people were trying to kill her. She should be safe now, or as safe as your average person who wasn't the former president's daughter was. Living her life. Doing her part to help other people. That was the life God had given her. And now someone was trying to take that away from her.

Kayla wasn't going to let them.

* * *

Conner knew why his handler had recommended he sever all personal ties before he went undercover. He'd been the perfect candidate—deceased parents, a sister he wasn't close with. No girlfriend or significant other to either break up with or ask to wait for him. But standing here with Kayla, Conner had to wonder why that was.

Sure, he'd been married to his work for a long time. Joining the Secret Service had been everything Conner ever wanted since he'd found out who those suited men standing around the president were.

Romance hadn't been part of his life. Especially when the woman he wanted had been young, impetuous in a way that had been both infuriating and adorable, and completely out of reach. The idea of a new Secret Service agent dating the president's college-age daughter was so unthinkable he'd been laughed at by his colleagues for even asking the question.

Fast-forward nearly a decade and Conner had seen Kayla a few times around town. He was pretty sure she never even knew he was there, as he'd made a point to avoid her. It wasn't a secret, even from Andis and his men, that he'd been Secret Service. He'd given them some privileged information about printing money to "buy" his way in, and Andis had accepted Conner as one of them. But distrust ran deep with criminals. They didn't fully trust him and probably never would.

Bringing down their organization from the inside would mean one less bad guy in the world.

But now the assignment was over. Pete had seen him. Conner would have to scrape together what he could and see if there was enough for a solid case—if they didn't kill him first.

After it was done, if Conner didn't wind up in witness protection, he'd have to give Kayla a call. The woman she had become was vibrant, despite the situation they were in.

Conner's gaze caught hers and he surveyed her face. Even with the smoke that now filled the air, she seemed to be doing okay. The fire department and the sheriff would show up soon, and then he'd leave her to her life while he took care of Andis.

He took a breath and it caught in his throat. Conner coughed it out. "We won't last much longer in here."

He scanned the room. Table and chairs. A fire extinguisher hung on the wall. That might come in handy.

Flames glowed orange between the door and frame, the wet towels now smoking.

"What do we do?"

Conner didn't answer. He waved Kayla to him. If this didn't go according to plan, he would regret spending this time with her and never saying the things that were in his heart. "Kayla—"

"No, no. Don't do that." She took a step back. "You're going to give me the 'I'll lay down my life to protect you' speech, aren't you? I know you, Conner. You'll always be a Secret Service agent, and I doubt there will ever be a day when you're in the same room as me that you won't feel like you're on protective detail." She sighed. "Because it's your job."

She was so far off the mark it wasn't even funny, but if he told her the truth—that he had seriously missed her—she would get embarrassed. So Conner walked to the window, put his back to the wall and peered out. They were on the second floor, but the awning above the store window downstairs was below them. If he smashed the window, they could use the awning—which would likely rip under their weight—to at least break their fall.

"Do you see them?"

Conner scanned the street. "No. And I don't see a fire truck or the sheriff either."

"What's taking them so long?" Kayla stepped over but, thankfully, kept well back of the window. "They should be here by now, shouldn't they?"

Conner didn't like this one bit. "I would have thought so."

The only reason for the delay he could think of was that someone at the sheriff's office had been paid off by Andis. Conner didn't like entertaining the idea that an officer of the law could be corrupt, but it did happen. It would hit Kayla hard, knowing her contacts in helping those women might not be completely aboveboard.

Boots in the hall, coming toward them.

"Firefighters." Kayla started for the door.

Conner grabbed her arm. "Wait a second."

"In there!" A man yelled.

Conner grasped the fire extinguisher. "Move to the side." If this wasn't firefighters, if it was Manny and his guys, Conner wasn't going to let them get a shot off before he could get Kayla out of there. He had his gun, but taking down the group would mean too many questions about who he was and why he'd been here. Not to mention the investigation would be over when Andis found out it had been Conner who'd killed his men.

He slammed the butt of the extinguisher against the window. The glass shattered, and he cracked out as much as he could, making sure he got everything on the bottom frame. "Let's go."

"You want to jump?"

The man in the hall yelled again. "Get it open!"

Conner grabbed Kayla's arm.

The door handle shifted, and someone banged against the door as though trying to open it with the force of his body.

He got Kayla to the window.

A gunshot blew a hole in the door beside the handle. Two. Three shots. Four.

"Go!"

He pushed her out.

Kayla landed on the awning, slid to the edge and rolled at the last second. She grabbed the edge and fell as the fringe ripped from the frame and she disappeared out of sight.

The door flew open.

Conner jumped. He tried to land on the awning as softly as possible, but his boots hit the material and went straight through. Conner prayed, for the first time in *years*, that he wasn't going to land on top of Kayla. When he hit the concrete, he rolled to disperse the force and bumped into Kayla's feet.

He looked up at her.

"That looked painful."

She wasn't wrong.

Kayla held out her hand, and he took it but didn't give her his weight as he got up. Then he let go and put his hand on her back to lead her away. He didn't need Manny and his men seeing them on the street. Just like he didn't need to know what her hand in his would feel like. Conner could have lived his life without that.

It would have been infinitely easier than knowing for sure now that her skin was soft and smooth and her smaller hand fit in his perfectly. That her warm fingers could lace through his when his were cold. No, he didn't need to know that. It wasn't going to be a comfort when he was on the run from Andis.

Conner sighed.

"Where do we go now?" Kayla asked. "I have no wallet, no keys. It's all in the office. I can't even get in my house." She pulled up short on the sidewalk, in the middle, right out in the open. Conner moved her to the alcove of a Laundromat that was closed.

"We'll figure it out, okay? Let's just get to my truck."

The air outside smelled like smoke. Where were the emergency services? Someone had to have called it in, and their call should have been responded to already. Conner didn't want to believe that the people who were supposed to protect Kayla and the others who lived in this town could be bought. That they'd intentionally allow an innocent to get hurt.

When they started walking again, she took his hand. Conner wanted to shake loose of her hold but he didn't. Still, she glanced at him. Conner saw it out of the corner of his eye. He couldn't answer the question that wasn't voiced. He wasn't in a position to do that, not when his world was one of lies and distrust that could get him killed, all for the sake of justice.

Kayla was everything he'd ever wanted, and Conner had to walk away from her.

But not yet.

Someone was behind them.

THREE

Kayla glanced over her shoulder and let out the breath she'd been holding. "Sheriff Johnson?" She turned and dropped her hands slowly. "I'm so glad you're here."

His hand rested on his gun, suspicion on his face at her and a strange man being in the street so close to her burning office. She didn't blame him. Kayla explained what had happened and how Conner had been there when the fire was started. How he'd helped her get out.

"And you don't know who was in the hall?"

"No." Kayla shook her head. Conner did, but she didn't.

"You didn't actually see anyone?"

"No, but we heard them." Her voice wavered with the questions that arose in her mind. Did he not believe they'd heard men talking in the hall? "They shot at us."

"I called the fire chief when I realized there was a fire that hadn't been reported." The sheriff glanced up at the building, flames now coming through the window they had jumped out of. "Seems strange no one called it in."

"I called it in," Kayla said. "I talked to Miriam."

The sheriff's eyes narrowed. "And you?" He motioned to Conner with a lift of his chin. "You got a name?"

"Conner Thorne."

Secret Service. She'd heard him say it a million times, but that was years ago. Kayla caught herself before she called Conner on it. His cover. Of course he had to stick with the story that he was no longer a special agent in order to protect himself and the investigation.

"Former Secret Service."

But he didn't mention being undercover. Didn't he trust the sheriff? If he didn't want to admit everything to the man, Kayla was going to trust he knew what he was doing. It was his job.

The sheriff opened his mouth to ask another question Conner probably didn't want to answer, so Kayla cut him off. She grabbed Conner's elbow and put her head on his shoulder. "He's with me."

Sheriff Johnson's eyes darkened.

"Conner is living in Samson now, and we knew each other at the White House. How many

people can say they have that kind of history?"
Kayla laughed, and it sounded false even to her
ears. She felt Conner's chest jerk with surprise.
It wasn't a lie, but she left it open enough the
sheriff had to draw his own conclusion. Everyone would put it together that they had known
each other way back when. He'd told her Andis
knew about their connection.

The sheriff cleared his throat. "I see." He was
handsome enough, Kayla supposed. Silver hair.
Good at his job, which made sense, as he'd been
doing it for thirty years now with no one ever
running against him. "You'll make sure she gets
home okay?"

"Sure thing."

That was it? Some man-to-man "take care of
the little woman" thing she didn't understand
at all. Kayla wanted to roll her eyes, but she'd
had enough of acting like a high school kid,
more than a lawyer could reasonably take for
one night. She needed to let go of Conner before
she started to believe her own ruse and got used
to holding on to him. Though, if they were dating for real, she'd be *way* cooler about it. Aloof.
Mysterious. A puzzle he needed to solve.

Conner's mouth had curled up. Kayla let go
of him, but was stuck beside him until the sheriff walked away.

"I actually didn't come here for the fire,"

Sheriff Johnson said. "Though I'll need formal statements from both of you after I talk to the fire chief. I have another case for you, Kayla. I wanted to tell you about this one in person, before I got the call about the break-in." He paused for a second. "I'll be talking to Miriam, because she didn't mention you being in danger, or the fire."

Kayla nodded. He waved her two steps away, and she joined him as he said, "Her name is Jan Barton. Got mixed up with a local guy she calls her boyfriend. I get the impression she needs somewhere to heal…and probably detox."

"Sure." Kayla's shelter was set up for that. The house manager she had hired was a registered nurse. "She's at your office?"

"Yep." The sheriff nodded. "I guess you have a ride."

"She does." Conner didn't look up from his phone.

She also had her own car, but neither man felt it necessary to point out that she was perfectly fine on her own. Or she would have been if not for tonight and the fact that she was still jumpy. Maybe it was just residual fear, but something was seriously not right.

The sheriff's brow had furrowed at Conner's statement. Why did she feel like the sheriff was not at all happy that Kayla had a "boyfriend"?

It wasn't like he'd ever given her the impression he was interested in her, so it could simply be fatherly concern. She'd have been polite, and flattered, but Sheriff Johnson knew some of her history. Not all of it, the way Conner did. The sheriff only knew she'd been the victim of an attack, and that was why she wanted to help women who needed safety. He'd even helped her set up the hotline.

So why was he bothered about Conner? Reservations would be justified if he knew Conner worked for Andis. If she could tell the sheriff Conner was undercover, it would allay his fears. When she looked up at Conner with the question likely in her eyes—he'd always been able to read her face—he shook his head.

The sheriff said, "Ms. Barton needs to get her things from her house while her boyfriend spends the night in one of my cells, and she needs to be clear of him before he gets out. Probably tomorrow, but it might be the day after."

Kayla nodded. "Does she want to get free?"

Sheriff Johnson shrugged one shoulder. "That's not my department. I find them, you help them." He smiled. "It's worked well so far."

"It has."

Sirens preceded the fire truck turning the corner. The rig drove past their huddle and stopped in the street in front of Kayla's office.

"I'll go run point with the chief and start a search for those men you saw. Let me know tomorrow how it went with Ms. Barton and I'll take your statements about what happened here then. In the meantime, get somewhere safe and I'll look into this. I'll also talk to Miriam."

Kayla watched him walk away.

"Huh."

She turned to Conner. "What? You don't like the sheriff?"

"Never met the man before tonight. Not sure he knows who I am, though he's going to look me up when he gets back to the office. By tomorrow he'll know my life story—or at least the one the Secret Service doctored for me when Andis looked me up. My identity as a disgraced agent is solid, so I'm not concerned. But the guy I'm pretending to be won't make him less worried about you. Probably more."

Kayla's stomach churned. "I'm not sure I like that you're getting close to men who would start a fire to try to kill someone. Whether their intended victim was you or me."

Conner placed his hands on her shoulders. "I'm not going to lie and tell you it isn't dangerous, but I'm good at what I do, Kayla. If there's trouble, I'll take care of it." He didn't add that now that his cover was blown, he was probably in more danger than ever.

Kayla didn't feel better in the least, but she was willing to cover it so he wouldn't worry about her when he left. "Let's go. Can we do that? I don't want to stay here if they're still around. Once I help Ms. Barton, I can go home and rest."

Conner waited for her to move first and then walked beside her. It was an old move she recognized. He'd fallen back into that protector/protectee relationship with her that would always color what was between them. And why was that? Maybe Kayla wanted to be the one to make sure he was safe, instead of him looking out for her all the time.

Why couldn't that be a thing?

Kayla stopped so fast she almost tripped on her heels.

"What? What is it?"

She pointed. "That's my car." At least, it used to be her car. Now it was a body with no wheels, smashed-out windows and spray-painted vulgar swirls all over it. "Someone trashed my car."

"Made sure you can't go anywhere and made it look like teenagers did it at the same time."

Kayla sighed. "We should tell the sheriff."

Conner turned and looked all around them, at the deserted parking lot to the rear of the street. Dim light. A back entrance. She knew what he saw, and there was no way he'd have let her come anywhere near a place like this back in the day. But she wasn't the current president's daughter anymore. No one cared who she was now.

At least, they hadn't until tonight.

"Let's get moving. You can report it tomorrow. Right now you need to get somewhere safe."

Kayla nodded and walked with him to his truck. He drove straight to the sheriff's office and waited outside while she went in and spoke with Ms. Barton. Kayla told the deputy on the desk about her car and had him relay that information to the sheriff in case it was relevant.

Jan Barton was the priority now. Kayla had seen bruises like that before, and the residue of what looked like a bad night. Way worse than the one she'd had this evening, even considering her office was toast and she smelled like smoke.

At least she could help Jan Barton, and then something good would come out of this night. Kayla had been through too much to settle for an old crush reappearing and taking up all of her thoughts and emotions. Conner had been everything she'd ever wanted.

Now all Kayla wanted to do was help other women so that none of them ever had to feel scared again. She knew what real fear felt like, and it had nearly crippled her—until someone had shown up to help her. That was who Conner was to her, the hero he'd been all those years ago.

She didn't need him in her life now. Kayla was too busy being that hero to others.

Conner waited outside Jan Barton's house. Kayla was helping her pack her things, but only after Conner had checked that the house was clear. The woman seemed nice enough, if beaten up and exhausted from a life lived in fear of her drug-addicted boyfriend. Now Conner was outside in case one of the boyfriend's friends showed up.

The two women exited the house, and Conner followed them to the truck. If not for the lack of a suit and earpiece, he'd have looked exactly like the Secret Service agent he was. But the casual clothes Andis's men wore meant they would never trust an expensive suit. That was Andis's dress code, not theirs. So Conner wore jeans and a shirt, like he did on a lot of his assignments. To blend in with the riff-raff.

Conner settled in the front seat and started the engine. He glanced back at Jan, just for a second, to make sure she was all right, but without scaring her by being an overbearing male.

His gaze snagged hers. Conner looked out the

front windshield again. Something was very, very wrong.

"Ready?"

Conner glanced at Kayla and put the car in Drive. "Sure."

She frowned, probably at the fact that his smile was completely fake. But Conner couldn't do anything else. This was the kind of person Kayla wanted to help? Conner couldn't decide which he disliked more, Kayla's being in the car with someone as off as Jan Barton or the fact that the sheriff brought these people to her.

"So where is this place?" If they were taking Jan to the property Kayla had bought, he needed to know where he was going.

"The motel on Fourth Street."

"A motel?"

"For tonight. I gave Jan a phone number, and she'll call the house manager tomorrow. That way, I'm never directly connected to the place." Kayla smiled. "Plausible deniability."

And yet if Andis had found out that Kayla was helping women…

His wife and daughter. Of course. Conner wanted to kick himself. Andis's wife and daughter had "moved away" a few months ago. What if Kayla had, in fact, helped them escape? The man might have lied to save face even while he began a search for them.

Was it that search that brought Manny to Kayla's office? Had that same hunt meant Conner had blown his cover tonight? She couldn't have known exactly how dangerous of a man Andis Bamir was. And if she had helped them, it gave the man a reason to want her dead. Andis wasn't bothered at all that his wife and daughter had left. In fact, it had only given him the ability to do what he did overtly instead of hiding it for their sake. If Andis felt anything, it was likely only that he'd been bested by Kayla because she had successfully helped them escape. He could want revenge.

Could he have been looking for them and kept it under the radar?

Conner needed to find a photo of Andis's wife and daughter online and show it to Kayla. If she had helped them, it would at least solve one mystery of the evening.

Kayla walked Jan to her motel room, and the two hugged. Still, even with that display of solidarity, Conner couldn't help thinking something about Jan Barton was…out of place. He shook off the idea. It had been a weird day for sure. Now it was the middle of the night and he needed to get Kayla home. She could get some sleep and he could sit outside in his truck and keep watch. Just in case.

After she'd buckled herself back in, Conner said, "Long day ahead of you tomorrow."

She nodded. "I'll have to make that statement to the sheriff and call my insurance agent, see how much work I can salvage. I back up at home, but my laptop is at the office. Maybe I've lost all my files from today." She sighed. "I really didn't need this. It'll be expensive to rebuild."

Conner pulled out onto the road. "I'm sure your father will help you out."

Kayla was his only daughter, and despite her wildness as a teen, he did dote on her. More so given that her mother had passed away. Some men distanced themselves from their loved ones after a loss. Conner had seen it in others— whether the loss was death or divorce didn't matter. It was all a type of grief to admit it was the end of what they'd thought their lives were going to be.

Kayla's father had been no different, though he had been an excellent president. Professional. Cordial to those who worked under him. Some presidents either ignored their Secret Service agents or treated them with outright disdain. It had been nice for Conner that the first president he had served under was a man who had respect for everyone, even those who could be construed as "beneath" him.

Conner hit the highway and pressed down on the gas, eager to get where they were going.

Kayla sighed. "Is it wrong that I don't want my father to help me?" Her voice was softer than it had been. "I mean, I'm a grown woman. If I told him what happened tonight, he would send a detail of Secret Service agents my way and insist they didn't leave my side until the threat against me had passed."

Conner didn't think that was a bad idea but got the feeling it wasn't what Kayla wanted to hear. "What do you want to do?"

"I'd like to live my own life and make my own decisions. I have to be strong enough to get through this on my own, or when a stiff wind blows through, I'll fall over and my life will disintegrate."

"I don't think a lack of strength has ever been your problem, Kayla."

She shifted in the seat. "Do you really mean that?"

Conner shrugged. "Of course."

Kayla slumped back down in her seat. "Sure, I guess."

"You don't think so?" He'd seen her weather things that would have broken most people, and yet here she was. A lawyer. A beautiful woman who could hold herself together when her office was burning and people were coming after them. Why couldn't she see that?

"You of all people know that what we show the world is usually not what's underneath the surface. No one wants to know the dark things, the parts of us that are terrified to show themselves."

She thought there was darkness in her? "Kayla—"

"Don't worry about it, okay? I do what I can for women who need help, and I like my job. I make a small difference, but it's still a difference." She glanced out the window. "It just has to be enough for me. That's what I'm struggling with."

Conner frowned. Perhaps it was fatigue making her doubt herself. He didn't see where she got the idea she didn't do enough. His whole existence right now consisted of pretending to be a bad guy—which meant he had to do bad things so they wouldn't figure him out—all for the chance to catch a real bad guy. He wasn't a force for good in the world, just justice.

Lights in his rearview mirror.

Conner switched the angle down so they didn't glare in his eyes and distract him.

The lights moved to the left and shone in his wing mirror. Some guy with a problem. Conner slowed a little and moved to the side of his lane so the person could pass if he wanted to. But he didn't.

The vehicle sped up, close enough to clip their back left bumper, and then backed off. Then sped up again.

Now they were on the right side.

"Not good."

"What?" Kayla shifted to face him. "What is it?"

"Just some idiot tailing us. Probably kids having fun with a lone truck on the highway." But he didn't believe it. After the night they'd had, there was no way it was a coincidence.

FOUR

Months ago a group of teens had tailed a woman on this highway, late at night. They'd taunted her before they ran her off the road. She'd hit a tree and suffered major injuries but didn't remember anything except that they'd driven a truck and jeered as they drove past her.

Kayla glanced back. The truck behind them could be the same truck of kids who'd hurt that woman. It was all she needed after her office was set on fire, and she'd had a long day before that happened. Now it was nearly midnight and she was exhausted.

Conner, on the other hand, was dressed like he lived for the rush of a late-night car chase. It was a far cry from the suits she was used to seeing him in, but it kind of worked. In a serious bad-boy way.

Kayla was in trouble—in more ways than one.

The truck burst forward and slammed into

their back bumper. Kayla screamed and grabbed the dash of Conner's considerably older vehicle. It would crumple under the newer, heavy-duty truck right behind them. Nearly on top of them.

"They're coming again!"

Conner gripped the wheel, his eyes intent. "Hold on."

"I am! What are you going to do?" She looked back. The truck had backed off, but it wouldn't be long before it came at them again. Could they outrun a more powerful truck? Kayla tried to remember if there were any side roads they could pull off onto. If so, they might escape, or the other truck could simply follow them. Stop them. Hurt them. Kill them.

The engine revved.

Kayla's knuckles turned white on the dash. Conner's truck jerked forward and he let off the gas. Metal scraped against metal. The tires caught on the road again, and he put his foot down. He drove like this was a mental exercise—a game of chess. They were either the king or simply pawns expendable in the grand scheme of the game. Kayla had never liked chess. She was much better with five-thousand-piece puzzles.

What was in Conner's head? He had to have a plan. He was a Secret Service agent. Only this threat was against both of them—not just her.

Kayla flipped the glove box open to see if there was a gun. It was stuffed with papers, and took two tries to get it closed again.

"You don't need a weapon."

"What about a phone? Mine is dead, remember? Give me yours and I'll call for help."

He shifted and dug it out of his jeans pocket.

"What's your handler under in your contacts?" Locked. "Wait…first give me your passcode."

"Call 911, Kayla."

She'd rather have a team of trained Secret Service agents, not the sheriff. Though the sheriff could probably get here faster. She'd seen the Secret Service in action so many times, but she hadn't wanted them there to protect her earlier. Not when it had been only her in danger. They were way past that now. For the second time that night, their lives were at risk.

Kayla pushed aside the questions that swirled in her mind—questions about why his phone was off-limits to her—and used the emergency feature to call for help.

No ringing sound.

She looked at the screen. Had the call connect—

Slam.

The truck lurched and Kayla dropped the phone. She needed two hands to hold on, or the next time they were hit, she'd slide out of her seat belt.

Kayla had no intention of dying tonight.

She checked behind them. The truck was neck and neck with them, and she could see a man inside. "It's not teenagers." She reached down and snapped up the phone. The call was still connected. "Hello?" Nothing. She tapped the screen. "Why is this thing not working?"

Conner gripped the wheel. "It's Andis's lieutenant. Manny."

"Manny." The man looked mean and was dressed...kind of the way Conner was. "So you know who he— Wait. That's who was in my hallway, wasn't it?" When Conner didn't answer, she said, "Can't you tell him to back off?"

"He's not going to back off. And no, it was one of his buddies earlier. He was probably outside. Now he's too busy trying to run us off the road so he can shoot us," he said through gritted teeth. "Manny must have followed us from your office and waited until now to try again."

"Give me your gun. I'll shoot out the window and get him to back off." The truck was on Conner's side, but she could make it work.

He didn't. "You're not shooting a gun right by my face. And you aren't going to hang out the window."

Okay, so she hadn't thought it through all the

way. What was wrong with winging it? This was a crazy situation. "So *you* shoot at him then."

"That's the best idea I've heard so far." He pulled his gun out. "Grab the wheel."

Kayla's hand darted out and she took hold of the steering wheel. He rolled the window down with the handle and air blew in. It dried out her contacts so that she had to blink moisture back over her eyes. Kayla held her breath as Conner fired off shot after shot.

The boom was so loud. It had been forever since she'd practiced with a weapon she'd forgotten it was that loud.

"Kayla!"

She glanced out the front window of the truck. The road bent to the left. She pushed the wheel toward Conner's door and they careened around the corner so fast the truck started to tip over.

Conner pulled his hand back in and the other vehicle backed off. Conner's truck scraped Manny's all down the side. He grabbed the wheel and she let go. But Manny didn't leave them alone. The truck angled into the back left side and clipped them.

Conner fought the spin, both hands on the wheel. The old truck shuddered and lost traction and they started to slide. Kayla screamed. She scrabbled around by her feet for the phone.

The truck was being pushed, forced off the road.

"He's going to kill us!" That was the point, but she didn't have to like it. They were going to die. The other truck would ram them one too many times and they'd flip. Conner's truck would crumple under the impact—with Conner and Kayla inside. There probably weren't even any air bags.

The sheriff would find them off the road, truck upside down. Bleeding. Dead.

Kayla tried to rein in her tendency to look at the catastrophic outcome first, but it was too hard. Things were bad. Really, really bad. They probably weren't going to make it. She was going to die in a truck with Conner Thorne and he'd never even know how much she'd cared for him for so long.

He'd been the light in her days. When she'd felt alone, he was in all the sweet memories she'd drawn up. On those dark days when she'd needed to feel the peace his presence brought, thinking of him had comforted her. Sure, he'd frustrated her to no end, and he'd never called. But he'd been it for her. She'd tried to date other guys, but no one had ever come close to even the dream of what could have been with him.

All that stuff about wanting someone who didn't know her was baloney. She wasn't even looking for anyone else.

The truck jerked and her forearm slammed down on the dash. Kayla screamed and lost her hold on the phone. It fell down by her feet and slid under the seat. *Help. God, help us.*

The truck jerked again, and they spun more. Off the side of the road and down a ravine. The truck hit a dip. Dirt sprayed and they lifted up. Airborne. Stars winked down at her as they rattled around in the cab, trying not to slam heads. Conner's face hit the steering wheel.

Kayla gripped the door handle, but it was no use.

The tree came out of nowhere. The truck slammed into it, and pain exploded through Kayla like a firework.

Conner blinked. He lifted a shaky hand to touch his face. His head pounded like a kick drum, and his hand came back wet with blood from his nose. The truck. He hated this truck anyway. The truck was probably almost totaled now, but he was alive.

Conner shifted. The movement sent pain shooting through his skull. Kayla was slumped in the corner against the door. Hair had fallen over one side of her face, and blood matted the blond strands against her skin. What breath Conner had left got caught in his throat. She was so pale she almost looked…

He pressed two fingers to the skin beneath her jaw. *Tha-thump. Tha-thump.* Low but steady. His body sagged and he moved his hand to touch her cheek. "Kayla." She needed to wake up. She had to open those eyes, those swirling blue depths that made him want to pull her close and draw strength from the way she looked at him. He needed to see her smile. The way her lips curled up and made it feel like the world melted away.

Conner had been undercover so long, starved for genuine conversation or real affection. Having Kayla here was like an oasis in the desert— but weren't those always the mirages of weary travelers? Dreams but not real. Just like the relationship he'd never have with Kayla, because he could never confess his feelings to her and keep her safe. This time together was a gift, but it wasn't their life. And it would be over soon.

Headlights lit the cab of the truck from behind. Conner glanced one more time at Kayla and then pulled out his gun.

Manny's truck stopped beside them, six feet of grass separating the two vehicles. Would he simply roll the window down and shoot them? Conner had to play this the right way, though he figured his cover was shredded now. Manny probably thought Conner was betraying them. He had to shift the man's focus. This had to be all about Kayla and who they had been to each other years ago. The only hope of keeping them alive was to make this about a woman and not about threatening Andis's business.

Kayla had implied to the sheriff that there was some kind of relationship between them, and he could do the same with Manny. Andis likely already knew he and Kayla were acquaintances, but not that Conner hadn't seen her again until tonight. If they thought Conner was starting a relationship with her, then he'd seem like he was just distracted, not working against them. Only interfering in Andis's activities—like warning her they were on their way—could get him in trouble.

It was the dance of every undercover assignment. Balancing who knew what and how much of the truth was necessary to strengthen the lie that was his whole life. He had to be the man the Secret Service had portrayed him as, the disgraced agent willing to share what he knew about counterfeit money in order to solidify his place as a bad guy.

Kayla would never know what it had meant to him to see her tonight. For her to realize the truth his own Secret Service colleagues couldn't know. Everyone he used to work with thought he'd been fired for misconduct. There was only one man in the Secret Service who knew Conner still worked for them—his handler, Greg.

A door slammed.

Conner looked at Kayla again and pulled on the handle.

Manny rounded the hood of his truck. Armed. If this didn't go right for him, it was going to go even worse for Kayla.

Her father wasn't doing well. Conner had asked his handler for updates after he'd read in the paper about a hospital stay for the former president. If Kayla was hurt—or worse—it wouldn't be good for the old man. Then again, it wouldn't be good when he found out his daughter was facilitating a battered-women's shelter either. Sure, she helped women and children feel safe, but Kayla had never once backed down when it was a fight she could win. He'd had that conversation with her father what felt like a lifetime ago now, and they'd agreed her stubbornness would get her in trouble one day.

Now it looked like that day had arrived.

"Let's go, Thorne. Andis will want to speak to you."

"Who says I'm going in? I have something to take care of first." Conner waved at the truck.

"Don't worry about that. She's coming, too.

Andis wants to talk to her, and you'd better be ready to explain why you spooked Pete. He tore out of that building so fast. Said you shot at him… Like, what on earth, man? You weren't supposed to be part of this."

"Part of what? Burning down a lawyer's office? She doesn't even represent criminals. And I didn't shoot first—Pete did."

"Being a lawyer isn't what Andis wants with her." Manny pulled out his gun. "And I wasn't asking."

"You could've killed both of us." He motioned behind him to the truck, where Kayla was still passed out. "You wanna explain how breaking into her office escalated to burning us out and trying to kill us?"

"You shouldn't have interfered. Pete freaked," Manny huffed. "The idiot decided to smoke you both out, so he got Earl on it. They figured you were there to get to the info faster and you'd be the one who'd give it to Andis instead. So the two of them caused a scene that's going to take days to iron out with the police."

Conner had wondered if Andis had some kind of arrangement with the local cops. Maybe not the sheriff himself. It could be someone who worked for him who was paid to look the other way, like the dispatcher who hadn't reported the fire. It was hard to be a good criminal with too many honest cops hanging around, and Andis wasn't above much—least of all bribery.

Manny lifted his chin. "So you can either tell me what that was about, or I can shoot you and tell Andis whatever I want. Kayla Harris goes to him either way."

"Not without me."

"Back off, Thorne."

"You don't touch Kayla Harris. No one does. Whatever Andis wants, I'll get it for him."

The sound of Kayla's screams still echoed in his ears. He was supposed to protect her, to give his life to save hers. Every second for the rest of his life, he would remember that feeling, that split second when he wondered if today was the day he would fail in his duty.

Conner folded his arms across his chest and said nothing.

"So you have betrayed us for a woman." Manny's laugh held no humor. "I wouldn't have believed it if I hadn't seen it with my own eyes."

"I haven't betrayed anyone."

"No, it's more like sold us out." Manny motioned to the truck with his chin. "She worth it?"

"We're not talking about this. What does Andis want with her?"

Manny's eyes flashed. For a second Conner saw an edge. Did he want to kill her, or did he want Kayla for something else? It seemed like he had a personal stake with Kayla, but how could that be? She was nothing to Manny but a job.

"She and I knew each other in the White House." Conner's tone suggested they were imbeciles for not having figured that out themselves. "Kayla and I go way back." Conner jerked his shoulder in the direction of his truck.

"Fine. Andis wants her brought in."

Conner didn't much care for Manny's tone. He needed to stake his claim. It was the only way these guys would accept his bone-deep need to keep her safe. Conner needed to at least try to remain in good standing with these guys and their boss if he was going to complete this assignment. Then he could get back in good standing with *his* boss at the Secret Service.

It meant everything to him that Locke knew he wasn't a disgraced agent.

Or it had. Until he walked into Kayla's office and saw her again.

Men like Manny and Andis understood possession. They understood lines men didn't cross, though often knowingly crossed them. The consequences would be real, and Manny knew that, too. Kayla was off-limits whether they were having a relationship or not. Manny, any of Andis's men and the boss himself had to know that this business didn't touch Kayla. There was no way he would let her get involved, even if she'd already done something inadvertently.

He stepped closer to Manny. "Kayla isn't going anywhere but with me."

It was a risky game, pushing Andis's number two. Conner was under him as far as the hierarchy was concerned, but they all knew what it was like being tied up in knots by a beautiful woman. Even bad guys fell in love. And it didn't matter what they thought about him being caught by her; it only mattered that they believed he'd fight for her.

Because he would.

Manny's gaze darted over Conner's shoulder. The truck door opened, then slammed shut.

Kayla.

"Conner?"

Conner didn't turn. Instead he watched Manny's eyes flare. He saw the man shift his stance, reacting to Kayla's presence in a way Conner didn't like at all. Manny glanced at Conner. "She's coming with me."

Conner stepped toward her. "I'm not going to let that happen."

Manny lifted his gun. Conner did the same, and they faced off as he moved to stand in front of Kayla. "Whoa," Kayla said. "I didn't see the gun."

Huddled behind him, she gripped the sides

of his jacket. With her head down, she'd be out of sight so that she wasn't a possible target. She remembered.

Conner faced his so-called friend and held the gun tight even as he guided them back. Out of the corner of his eye he saw Kayla's hand trace the hood of the truck as they went.

"Kayla isn't going anywhere." Except where Conner put her, behind cover so he could keep her safe.

Manny fired at them.

FIVE

Conner's body jerked and he fired back. Kayla ducked. She couldn't move until he gave her the all clear. She'd make herself a target. Air hissed and she realized the sound was coming from between her own teeth clenched together. In the second after he fired, Conner dropped down beside her. Finally. It had seemed more like a minute as time stretched out. It always did when the expanse between heartbeats was so precious and she didn't know if she would get another moment or if she would be dead.

He pushed her toward the door. Past it. Kayla stumbled. A rock lay beside her hand. Kayla hurled it over the truck at the man who'd ducked behind his own vehicle. The side window smashed. Bull's-eye.

Conner shoved her into the footwell on the passenger side and climbed onto the seat, keeping his head down. It took a few tries, while she wondered if they needed to abandon the truck and run for it, but the engine caught. How old was this vehicle?

Conner wound the window down with the handle and fired twice. Kayla had to clap her hands over her ears. It had taken all the strength she had to walk over to him, but she hadn't been able to leave it alone. The man was going to kill Conner—she'd seen the intent in his eyes. Manny, Conner had called him. Cold eyes, and that wicked stare.

Allowing herself to be protected was a reflex, especially with Conner. She couldn't help falling back into the dynamic of him as the agent and her as the charge who was to be shielded at all costs. She wanted to be strong. For once she wanted to be the one who got to choose to put her life on the line protecting someone else. Not to die but to prove that the person she cared for had value and was worth saving.

Curling up on the floor of the truck hurt like she'd been the ball in a pinball machine, slammed into every available surface. But she had to hold her ground if she was going to help keep Conner alive. His job was the priority here.

"Lean over and hit the gas."

What? Kayla had to turn around and contort her body painfully, but she found the gas pedal with her fingers and pressed it down. The truck roared and launched backward. Conner grabbed the wheel but didn't look out the windows. Gunshots peppered the front hood, and the window smashed.

Bang. "Seven." *Bang.* "Eight." *Bang.* "Nine. He's out." Conner sat up. He grabbed the wheel with both hands and she moved her fingers off the gas a second before his foot slammed into it. "He'll have to reload. Never did like to wait for a clear shot. Hold on." The truck lurched up the hill, going backward. Conner spun the wheel and threw it into Drive.

The tires hit paved road and the ride smoothed out.

Kayla pressed a hand against her chest. Her arm was heavy, and her shoulder hurt. Not to mention her head. "Wait. You were shot."

"Hit my vest." He patted his chest.

Kayla squeezed her eyes shut. *Thank You, Lord.*

Her face was sticky, and Conner's didn't look much better than hers felt. Was his nose broken? They probably needed a hospital. Could Conner go to the emergency room when he was undercover with the best-known criminal in the county? She didn't know what the Secret Service's policy was on that. Maybe she should call Locke later. The special agent who had been Conner's supervisor should be able to shed some light for her on the dos and don'ts of undercover operations.

What were they going to do now? Andis Bamir "wanted" her, whatever that meant. Conner hadn't been okay with that, which was fine with her. He knew them. But now she and Conner were on the run.

Thank You, Lord, for protecting us. For keeping us alive. Help us out of this and neutralize Andis. Help Conner finish this job. She wanted him to be done, and safe, as much as she wanted Andis and his operation out of commission.

Only that would mean Conner's time here would be over.

And then he would leave.

Conner lifted his hand, then slammed his palm down on the steering wheel. "Phone."

Kayla blinked at his abrupt order and then looked around. She fished it from under the seat and handed it to him. Conner made a call. "Because it's done." He paused. "I'm blown."

Kayla directed Conner to her house and he parked down the street. When she glanced at him, he said, "In and out, two minutes. Got it?"

She nodded, so he continued, "I don't think Manny followed us. I shot out one of his tires, but we're not taking chances one of the others isn't watching your house. Get your stuff."

Conner scanned the area as he strode down the front walk. He couldn't surround her, so he covered her as best he could. The tiny one-story house was like a fairy-tale setting. Flowers everywhere, colors that probably looked fantastic in the daylight. Spring had sprung in her yard, taking him back to memories of his childhood. He'd been in fourth grade and a lost neighborhood puppy had crawled under the fence into their yard. The puppy had dug holes all over the grass, eaten half his mother's flowers and then thrown up. After that it'd been so exhausted it slumped on its side and took a nap.

That was how Conner had found it.

And picked it up.

And hid it in the shed barely in time before his mom came home and freaked out because her magazine-worthy backyard had been destroyed.

He'd taken the blame, and the grounding, and managed to hide the puppy for another two weeks before his dad figured out what was going on.

And he'd replanted everything by himself.

Kayla put her hand on his arm, jolting him from his thoughts. Focus. He had to focus, or one or both of them would end up dead.

"I hope you can pick a lock, because I don't have my keys."

Finally, something he could do that was easy. Conner got them inside and had Kayla wait by the front door while he cleared the house. "Okay. We're good for the moment." He headed toward the door. "Pack your bag for a couple of days, but do it fast."

Kayla stared at him. Eventually, she nodded, then trailed down the hall.

Whatever that had been, he was glad she wasn't arguing. Conner glanced around while he waited. He really liked her house. It was... homey. Kind of girlie for his tastes, but then, she probably wouldn't like his brown couch and the fact that his house smelled like the previous owner's dog. But he wasn't in this line of work for the sweet accommodations. Thugs didn't live in expensive condos or cute little houses.

He should hurry her up so they could leave. It wasn't safe for her, and they needed to get out of there as soon as possible. But he figured that despite what had happened, and maybe because of it, he shouldn't say it. She'd done the right thing, and they'd survived that encounter with Manny, but she was at ease now. He didn't want to spoil it, even if he was still completely tuned in to what was happening.

Just in case Manny—or any of Andis's other men—showed up to try to kill them again.

Conner rubbed his chest where the bullet had

hit his vest. The latest in body armor, it didn't look obvious under his shirt, but now Manny would know without a doubt. Only a cop would wear protection.

"Let's go, Kayla!"

She rushed down the hall with a bulging tote bag over one shoulder. "I figured packing light was better."

"It is." He grabbed her hand and they strode to the front door. He scanned the street, the other houses, everything, but half his attention was on the feel of her hand in his. So soft, especially compared to the Sig in his other hand. He could hardly describe how it felt in his chest to have her close. To be touching her, even in this small way.

And she would never know it.

Fifteen minutes later he had them checked into a cheap motel that didn't require his ID or ask questions.

Kayla dumped her tote on the bed and hissed, then brought her elbow around so she could peer at it. "Ouch. Looks about as bad as your nose."

Conner caught hold of her hand. He turned her so he could see the road rash that covered her elbow. "Did the truck do that?" The passenger door was all bent plastic and sharp edges. It was good she hadn't suffered worse.

"Conner, you know your nose is probably broken, right?"

He shrugged one shoulder. "Not the first time." She wet a washcloth in the bathroom sink and he held it to his nose. "Okay, now it hurts." He tried to smile, but she didn't return it.

Conner tossed the washcloth on the bed and tore open a packet of gauze so he could clean her elbow for her. Kayla pursed her lips and blew air out.

He winced. "Sorry."

She shook her head. "Don't be, not when your nose looks like that. You're the one who got shot. I don't know why you're worried about my elbow. We got through it together, Conner, but if you hadn't been at my office, I'd have died tonight."

"I wouldn't go that far." His presence had escalated things. "Kayla—"

"Don't downplay it. I got out of the truck to help, which didn't go so well, but you did so much more." She leaned back and pulled her arm from his grip.

"If you really knew the kind of man he is, you would have stayed in the truck where I *left you* and let me deal with him." Conner could feel the blood coming from his nose again but ignored it. "They were going to take you to their boss, Kayla. A man you do not want to meet. A man who uses people and then makes them disappear when he's done. I don't want you anywhere near him, and I definitely don't want you drawing even more attention to yourself."

Kayla grabbed the washcloth and pressed it against his upper lip. "They already know who I am." Her words were soft, and he saw what looked like grief there. She had suffered a loss tonight, even if it was only a loss of her peace of mind and the sense of safety most people took for granted that had gone up in flames along with her computer and all of her files.

He said, "You don't want to be someone they remember."

"I know. That's why I always worked so hard to be someone *you* remember."

Conner stared. Kayla stared right back, not scared. Not nervous. Nothing but a carefree hope that meant she had apparently forgotten they'd nearly died that night. Didn't she care that Andis was after her? Or did she just trust him that much to protect her?

Kayla saw an opportunity and jumped in with two feet. He admired it about her, even while it had driven him almost nuts watching it and knowing he could only protect her from afar. He could never be the man she chose to protect her for the rest of her life. "Kayla—"

She swayed sideways, far enough that she

slumped toward the floor. Conner grabbed her before she fell and looked at her face. Her eyelids fluttered. She raised a hand to her forehead. "Conner."

He lifted her in his arms and carried her to the armchair. Concussions could be tricky things, and he wanted to wait a couple of minutes to see if she came around before he called an ambulance and completely blew their cover at the motel. It could just be exhaustion and the sudden absence of adrenaline.

Kayla made a low noise in her throat and burrowed into him before he could settle her onto the chair. "Missed you."

Conner's phone buzzed in his back pocket. He checked on Kayla, then moved away and pulled out his cell. The screen went black and then illuminated again. Greg was calling back.

Conner answered. "I'm okay."

Greg exhaled loudly. "Thank You, God." He muttered the words and then said, "When you didn't call back, I was starting to get worried."

"Good news is the body armor works." He kept his voice down so he didn't wake Kayla. "Bad news is I need you to call a doctor and find out what to do with a possible concussion." He explained what had happened and Kayla's almost passing out.

"I'll find out."

"Thanks, Greg." Conner sank into a chair. His handler had been a colleague before tonight. Now he was a lifeline. "Manny will be after me, trying to clean up the mess the guys made. Kayla is still loose, and Andis will want to speak with her."

"You've lost your in with them."

"They shouldn't have kept this business with Kayla from me," Conner said. "They must have known I knew her, so they never said anything. Probably figured I'd step in, which I did anyway." He blew out a breath. "This whole thing is a mess. They're never going to trust me now that I put a woman over what Andis wants."

Greg didn't comment either way. They were both Secret Service agents and Kayla was the daughter of a former president. There was nothing to say.

Greg broke the silence. "How much of the case is salvageable?"

"I'm not leaving until Kayla is safe. If we can make a case on what I've collected, we should move forward."

"It isn't enough. They'll want more than that before they go for an arrest warrant." Greg paused, and Conner knew he wasn't going to like what Greg would say next. "They want you to find out where he's printing the money. All or nothing, Conner. They want the whole organization to come down. After the money quit flowing, there was some question over whether you'd spooked them, but I don't think that's it."

Conner sighed. Weeks after he'd talked his way into Andis's operation, the money had stopped coming in. For some reason, the counterfeit operation had ceased. And no one was talking about it.

"Whatever the reason," he said, "I think it has something to do with Kayla. They came after her hard. If I hadn't been there, she'd be with Andis. A hiker would have found her floating in the river three days from now." Conner could barely think about it, but it was a hard world he lived in. One he was going to keep Kayla protected from at all costs.

Conner sighed. "So keep her safe and find out where Andis was printing money, and at the same time, figure out why the counterfeiting suddenly stopped."

"No one ever said undercover work was easy," Greg said. "But I do have a team on standby."

"No. The team doesn't know I'm undercover. They think I betrayed the Secret Service. There's no way they'll trust me, and I have to finish this. It's my job."

"And it's Kayla's safety."

"She's good." Greg didn't have to remind

him. Conner would deal with the threat to her. "We're good."

But what if something happened to her because he'd assumed he could handle it? Conner squeezed the bridge of his nose. "I want the team in the area on standby. I don't want my identity leaked—I just want available backup."

"Done. What about local cops, the sheriff?"

"I trust the Secret Service more."

Greg said, "Stay safe. I'll get a medical opinion on concussions."

"Thanks." Conner wasn't taking any chances. If he was going to keep Kayla safe and finish this assignment, it would take everything he had. "And, Greg?"

"Yeah, Conner?"

"Get me a picture of Andis Bamir's wife and daughter. I need to ask Kayla something when she wakes up."

SIX

Kayla looked around and pushed back the covers. Conner was asleep in the armchair. He'd woken her a couple of times to make sure she was okay. Something about doctor's orders. Then he'd gone back to the armchair and dropped off to sleep in an instant while she'd lain there with her brain spinning. After that she'd stared at the ceiling listening to his soft snore.

It took two cups of nasty motel coffee before her brain kicked in and she quit being so disoriented. Despite his not seeming to mind sticking around and taking care of her, Conner needed to wake up. She couldn't bear to rouse him, though. He looked exhausted. Kayla took a shower, hoping the noise woke him at the same time she prayed it didn't.

When she came back out, he was still sleep. He'd put his jacket on the back of a chair and discarded his boots. His hair was rumpled, and the shadow of a beard covered his face below his swollen nose and the tiny strips of bandage that he'd put over it. That looked like it hurt. Kayla filled a cup of coffee for him and set it on the end table as the need to wake him evaporated.

But what else could she do?

She wished she was at home, where she could see her things. Her parents' wedding picture. The framed photo of her father being sworn in as the president. Kayla waltzing with the Italian ambassador. Conner. A candid photo, one of the few in which neither of them had their guard up. Maybe it was better that they were in a motel and not where he could see that she still had a copy of it. Thankfully he hadn't noticed it when he was searching her house.

It was taken at a Christmas party, so long ago she'd still had that nose ring. Her head was tipped back as if she'd been laughing. Conner had a smile in his eyes, and all of his attention was on her. Someone had snapped a rare moment when they hadn't been fighting.

Before everything had gone wrong.

Before she'd thought it was a good idea to slip free of her Secret Service detail and go to a brand-new club. Before a man had dropped a drug into her drink and she'd gotten dizzy. The man had walked her to the back entrance, probably knowing if he used the front, someone would recognize her.

He'd almost made it, too. Until Conner showed up. She barely remembered what had happened because of the drug's effects, but she would never forget the look on Conner's face as he stared into her eyes and asked her if she was okay. He'd been furious. She was also pretty sure he'd beaten up the guy who'd tried to abduct her, because he'd had swollen red knuckles the next day.

Just doing my job.

She'd tried to talk to him about it, to thank him for saving her, but he'd brushed it off as no big deal. Duty. Like there wasn't a well of emotion between them. Like she was nothing but a charge to him. Kayla had applied for law school the next day. Maybe to make him miss her, and maybe a little part of her had wanted to make something of herself so that he'd have to face the fact that she was somebody. Not just the president's daughter, but *somebody*.

She'd hardly seen him after that and definitely hadn't spoken to him. She'd found faith thanks to a roommate who didn't quit sharing with her about the love of God.

Kayla smiled to herself, perched on the end of the bed and sipped more coffee. She knew who she was now: not just a lawyer but a child of

God, as well. *Beloved.* It shouldn't matter what Conner saw in her now, but part of her relented to the fact that it did.

Conner's phone chimed. Kayla turned in time to see him jump out of the chair and whip his gun from behind his back.

"Is the phone trying to kill you?" She brought the cup to her lips, feeling a smile there.

He blinked and his dark eyes came to her. "We don't joke about threats."

She swallowed. Apparently that had been a bad idea. "Sorry."

Conner stowed his gun back in his shoulder holster and picked up his phone. And the coffee. He drank half a cup with his eyes on his phone while he tapped and swiped. "Kayla, come here." He wiped his mouth with the back of his sleeve.

"Why? What is it?"

He didn't move. His expression didn't change. "It's the email I was waiting for. Now come here."

Kayla walked over. He handed her his phone. On screen was a picture of a woman and child. "Sofija and Lena. Why do you have a picture of—"

"I asked my handler for a picture of Andis's wife and daughter, the ones who disappeared. After you told me about the work you do helping

women, it struck me this might be why Andis
wants to talk to you." *And then kill you.* Neither of them said it, but it hung between them
nonetheless. Conner said, "Did you help them
get away?"

"It was a bad situation. She was being beaten,
and she was scared for her daughter's life."

"I believe you. Kayla, it isn't a bad thing that
you helped them. But it likely is the reason
you've hit Andis's radar and why he sent men
to flush you out of your office and bring you in."

Kayla handed him his phone. She didn't know
what to say. Each day she prayed for every
woman and child she'd ever helped. No matter
how many there were, Kayla never forgot them.

A few had left town; a few had rebuilt their
lives in town and were thriving—some even
in new, loving relationships—but a couple of
the women had gone back to the men who hurt
them. They were never far from Kayla's heart.
Once in a while she got an email on a separate web-based account she kept active. But not
often. If Sofija had sent her an email, though,
Andis might be able to use it to find her.

"I have to get to my office. Or what's left of
it."

"That's it?"

"What do you want me to say? Sofija and
Lena are long gone, and that's where they need

to stay. If I can get to my computer first, then I can make sure he won't ever find out about the email account and they will stay safe for good."

Conner leaned in. "Andis won't stop. He'll send Manny or someone else to bring you in. And they won't be nice about it. He'll make you talk."

"There won't be anything to say. I don't know where she is." She folded her arms. "Maybe while we're in town I'll go to the sheriff and give my statement. I can tell him it was Andis who destroyed my office and tried to kill me. Get him arrested."

"You should do that, because the sheriff will likely follow up."

"I can leave your name out of it so you don't have to worry about Andis learning you're still Secret Service." She lifted her hands and let them drop by her sides. He was freaked out— for her. "Don't worry about me, Conner. Just finish your job. That's why you're here."

"It's not why I'm *here*. With you. Why do you think I came to your office as soon as I heard them say your name? They know we know each other—we just have to use that to our advantage. Stick together."

She could see him reasoning out the problem, the way his eyes looked at her but didn't really see her. He didn't get it. He didn't understand that she was trying to help him, to let him off from protective duty so he could concentrate on work. She could call her father, get a detail of Secret Service agents. Conner could move on. He didn't need to stay with her.

Conner touched the skin of her elbows with his warm hands. "You think I'd let you swing in the breeze for my job?"

Kayla shrugged. "I told you that you don't need to protect me. It's not your job anymore." Yet he was here with her. He'd looked out for her. Taken a bullet for her.

Why did that make her want to cry?

"I know you don't need me, Kayla." There was hope in his eyes. Where was that coming from? "Things have changed for both of us. Life has changed, but it's brought us here. Together."

What was he saying? "Conner, I really have to get to my office and then see the sheriff." Stopping Andis from getting what he wanted was the most important thing.

They were supposed to just go their separate ways? Sure, it was probably logical. If her life wasn't in danger. If he didn't have to protect her from Andis. But Conner wasn't going to just watch her walk away into the sunset. It would hurt to be around her and know they could never be together. If he could help her, for the sake of what was between them, he would do it.

She'd said she missed him. The sweetest two words Conner had ever heard, and it didn't seem like she even remembered she had said them.

"Conner."

Yep, he was staring at her like a weirdo and not saying anything. "You want to call in the Secret Service, that's fine by me. But you don't leave my sight until either you have a protective detail or your life is no longer in danger."

"Conner!"

He'd just have to protect her regardless. He could keep watch on her without her even knowing he was there. If she wanted to think that was the better option, fine. He wasn't going to argue about it. He wasn't in the position to change things, but how hard would it be for her to just admit she wanted to see what could be between them?

"This isn't an argument, Kayla—it's how it's going to be. We stay together until someone comes to relieve me. You want to call them in, fine. Do it."

Okay, so he was baiting her into making a move but that wasn't the point. Whether or not it made him feel better about her not wanting to be around him wasn't the point either. The point was that she would be safe.

Conner walked his mug to the tiny motel coffeepot and set it down. If she wanted someone else to protect her, that was fine, but he didn't have to act as if he liked it.

He grabbed his keys. "Get your stuff. Let's go."

He could take her to her office. She'd have to follow his lead, just like any other protectee. That's what they were, after all. Just a Secret Service agent and the former first daughter. He'd thought they had something more than that, but apparently he was wrong. When it was important, when it counted that they look out for each other, she wanted someone else.

They rode in silence to her office, thankfully free of gawkers, who kept regular office hours. It was just past six in the morning, so the only person on the street was a jogger gazing up at the second floor's burned-out windows. Conner didn't stop; he drove right past the building. He saw her shift and look at him out of the corner of his eye, but he didn't say anything. She knew the drill. He turned the corner and parked on a secluded street where they wouldn't be seen and where they could exit in either direction.

"Don't get out of the car until I let you out."

Kayla sighed. When he opened the door, she climbed out. They trudged in silence to the building, then up the stairs. He was in hyper-awareness mode, and she couldn't help but fall into step with it. It was who they were. Always had been, always would be.

Kayla pushed open the door to her office but didn't enter. He had to check it out first. But it was empty.

"Tread carefully."

The whole place had been cordoned off, presumably by the sheriff and the fire department. They'd all gone home now. She probably had a stream of voice mails on her home phone, as she did on her cell, reminding her to come into the sheriff's office to make a statement.

Her office was a complete mess. Black soot covered every charred inch, including warped wood and shattered light fixtures. The walls looked like fire had melted the paint, so hot it had dripped down to pool on the floor.

"Where's your computer?"

Kayla looked around. The top of the desk was only slightly less charred than the rest of the room, but her laptop wasn't there. She'd had it on her when she came back to the office, but in the padded backpack she used to transport it to and from home.

She circled the desk and scanned the floor for her backpack. It looked pretty well protected, hidden behind the desk. *Thank you, Dad, for the expensive desk.* If she had planned on telling him about any of this, she'd have sent flowers for that. Instead he'd never know. She could call Locke, get a detail here. They could keep it hush-hush, and her dad didn't need to find out her life was in danger. His heart wouldn't be able to take the strain.

"Superficial damage. It's more cleaning up than repair work from the looks of it."

She glanced back at Conner and gave him a small smile. "That's good. I'll have to call my insurance guy, get the ball rolling on renovations."

Kayla pulled out the laptop and set it on the blackened desk. She lifted the lid. "Oh, no." The buttons were all melted, and the screen had warped. "This isn't good. I don't remember my passwords—I make my browser do that—and this email isn't linked to anything else so I can't reset it. Now I have no way to warn Sofija."

"True." His voice was soft. "But now neither does Andis."

Kayla sighed. It was a really good thing she'd bought fireproof file cabinets and a fireproof safe. She should have put her computer in the safe or grabbed it when that bottle flew through the window. It was like toast cooked on high and forgotten about.

Conner took up so much headspace with

his questions. And his presence. He made her shiver, even though she didn't want to react to him at all, let alone like that. The bad-boy thing seriously worked.

"Huh."

Kayla sighed. They needed to be done now. She had her laptop, and there wasn't anything else to do right now, was there? Unless she went to the computer store to see if any of the information could be salvaged. Still, she said, "What is it?"

He'd turned to the corner and her high cabinet. "Right here." He pushed aside two books and pulled something from the top corner of the shelf. A collection of wires came out, attached to— "This looks like a tiny camera, maybe even a recording device, meant to transmit back to whoever set it up. Audio, video. Why would this be in your office?"

Kayla blinked and stepped back. Could they see her now, or had it fried like her laptop? "Who could have put that there?"

He broke the camera off the wires and held it out, but Kayla didn't take it. She didn't even want to touch it. She didn't want to think about who they were or what they'd seen and heard in her office. Her thoughts crystallized into perfect clarity as Kayla realized—

"Someone has been watching you."

She couldn't move. "Andis?"

"He does use technology sometimes, but why listen and watch if he intends to bring you in? There would have had to be a trigger that made him make a move now if it was him listening."

Kayla shook her head. "So, then, someone else? But who? Who could possibly want to spy on me at work?" The breath whooshed from her lungs in a rush that left her dizzy. "Are these in my house, too?"

Conner's face hardened. "I don't know, Kayla."

SEVEN

Conner tossed the surveillance device on the desk. He didn't figure Andis or any of his men had planted it. Covert operations weren't their style, though he'd seen them use it to entrap people before. Mostly when they were owed money.

Someone wanted access to Kayla's life without her knowledge. Could it be her father watching over her? Or the Secret Service? Surely they'd have let her know they were bugging her office.

"We shouldn't stay long," he said. "We don't know how close Manny is behind us." He glanced at her, taking in all that pale skin and those big eyes that eclipsed her whole face. The fact that he cared about her made it a thousand times worse, not better, that he was her entire security detail.

At least for now.

If he called in the standby team he'd be able to

leave her with professionals whose lives weren't tied up in what happened to her. Kayla had been through way too much so far for his peace of mind. It likely wouldn't let up until this was over, but at least he could minimize the danger to her.

She clutched the laptop to her chest now. "You have that 'you helpless woman, me big strong agent' look on your face again." Her lips curled up on one side, not like she was amused. More like she thought it was cute. "You can't wrap me in Bubble Wrap, you know."

"It's worth a thought, at least." Conner didn't mean it. Okay, maybe a little. Keeping her safe was creeping up his priority list like an incessant spider, now neck and neck with closing the case against Andis. His obligations tore him in two different directions. If the man wasn't targeting Kayla, Conner would have chosen to take her far from here and given up the case. But bringing down Andis would ensure Kayla's safety.

He scanned Main Street outside the window. Businesses had opened for the morning, and the coffeehouse seemed to be over its before-work rush. A steady stream of traffic meandered in both directions, but it was the blue truck that caught his eye. Manny was in town.

"New tires."

"What was that?"

Conner turned. He strode toward her, handing over his cell phone as he did. "Take my phone." He gave her his code. "My handler is listed as Mom. And give me yours." She'd charged it at the hotel, and kept it on her since, but the numbers stored on his were their lifeline. "Sit tight here for as long as you can. If you don't feel safe, find somewhere that is. Do whatever you need to, okay? Call the sheriff if you don't like what you see, but if you need something, call Greg."

"What do you mean…?"

Conner was already in the hall. No one was there, nor was anyone on the stairs or in the parking lot. He skirted the building and sprinted toward the pharmacy. This morning he and Manny were supposed to lean on the pharmacist, and he figured that was exactly what Manny had planned.

It was probably a trap, but he wasn't going to let Manny hurt the pharmacist just because he wanted to draw Conner out. That was why he'd left Kayla behind. She could call the sheriff, get protection for herself. The pharmacist had no one.

The man hadn't been paying Andis his "protection" money the way the other businesses in town did. He couldn't afford it, because his grandson had leukemia.

Conner hadn't been sure how to help the situation. Manny was ruthless, and Conner couldn't intervene in stuff like that without Andis realizing he wasn't one of them. The last time this situation came up, his hands had been tied, so he'd managed to get a gig at a construction site instead.

Bodyguard duties for the contractor—a man who owed Andis—was a better use of his Secret Service skills. But that wasn't exactly what it had been.

He'd kept his eyes and ears open and made sure the man wasn't skimming off his income. Andis wanted to get paid as soon as possible, which meant Conner's presence had been more about intimidating the man into making as much money as possible.

At least he hadn't had to resort to assault.

Conner blew out a breath as he ran. Helplessness was not a feeling that he liked. Kayla would be okay, but if he didn't bring down Andis, the town wouldn't be. Hardworking people were being pressured into making payments to a mobster in exchange for being left alone.

Manny's truck roared down the street and pulled up in front of the pharmacy. Usually he was somewhat discreet, using the back parking lot. Today the man clearly wanted to make a statement.

Conner's stomach knotted as he watched Manny enter the pharmacy in broad daylight carrying a shotgun. Manny was happy to make an example of the pharmacist, making Conner look soft in comparison. He'd pulled Manny back from going too far and permanently hurting someone on more than one occasion.

The door opened again. Manny dragged the pharmacist off the curb and onto the street. A car swerved, honked and then sped off. People screamed. A lady pushing a stroller started to run, dragging her tiny leashed dog away from them. Doors slammed. Some people rushed to get away, while others gawked, digging phones from pockets to videotape the situation.

"Get out of here!" Conner couldn't protect a whole crowd. One gunshot in their direction could hurt many, depending on what kind of shells Manny had in that thing. Didn't they know they were close enough to get hit?

Manny shoved the pharmacist to his knees and pointed the shotgun at the back of his head. He yelled something Conner couldn't hear. The pharmacist went white and said something back. His hands trembled as he lifted them in surrender. This wasn't about him, but it didn't matter. He was going to get hurt in the cross fire with absolutely no idea it wasn't a turf war or two bad guys fighting. No one here, except for Manny, knew about the Secret Service. Conner didn't exactly hang out with people in town and share his résumé or stories of being fired from the president's detail.

Only Kayla knew the whole truth, and she was the only one he wanted to spend time with. He needed to get this done and get back to her.

Conner pulled his gun and held it with two hands low in front of him as he crossed the parking lot to the street as fast as he could.

"Manny!" Not waiting for the man's attention to shift to him, Conner aimed his gun. The pharmacist probably didn't expect a war between Manny's guys, but that's what it was going to be.

"I knew you'd come out to save him." Manny grinned. "Now you're a dead man, Conner." He lifted the gun.

"Don't do it," Conner yelled. "Put it down." He should arrest this man, but then he'd never bring Andis down.

"I knew you were still an agent. I knew it! And now I'll prove it to Andis. Prove you aren't the golden boy he thought you were." Manny had no sense of self-preservation. Didn't he know he was on camera?

They faced off on the street, the pharmacist on his knees between them.

"Put the shotgun down."

"So you can shoot me?"

Conner held his aim. "If I was planning on it, I'd have done it already. Now let the pharmacist go back in his store. This is about you and me."

"And Kayla Harris. Where is she?"

"Safe." *Please be safe. Please be calling the sheriff before this escalates any further.* Conner wasn't sure he was going to be able to contain the situation. Hopefully, Kayla was praying, too. He hadn't gotten the chance to ask her about that cross which hung around her neck, the one that reminded him of the cross his mom had worn.

"Bring her out. Let's have a party."

"I don't think so, Manny."

Andis's man held the barrel against the pharmacist's head. Sweat ran down the sides of the old man's face, all caught on camera by this crowd of idiots hanging around in the line of fire. The sheriff needed to get here fast before people lost their lives.

"Let the old man go and I'll go with you."

"Kayla Harris, too."

"Whatever you want, Manny." Like he was going to let that happen. "Just let him go and we'll get in your truck."

* * *

Kayla leaned against the wall where she was able to see out the window, in almost the exact spot where Conner had seen whatever had made him rush out like that. Okay, so she understood he had priorities, and with the scene now taking place on the street, she was seriously glad he'd gone down there.

Especially when something terrible was about to happen. *Lord, protect those people.* She wasn't too worried about herself. Everyone's attention was on the street, not on her huddled up here by herself. Kayla had to stay put, but used Conner's cell to call the sheriff's personal number.

"Sheriff Johnson." He sounded breathy.

"This is Kayla Harris. You have to get to Main Street right—"

"Two men with guns facing off?"

He was going to find out when he got there. "It's Manny. He works for Andis. The other is Conner."

"Are you safe? Out of the way?" When she said yes, she was, he answered, "Good. I've got two deputies with me, and I'm almost there. I need to let you go."

Kayla heard the click on the line and exhaled the breath she'd been holding. Conner and the sheriff both wanted no casualties and, ideally, no one hurt. They were trained, and she was a lawyer who'd taken some self-defense courses. So long as she hung out here and stayed hidden, she would be okay.

Totally safe.

A floorboard in the hall creaked.

A siren sounded for a second, and blue-and-red flashing lights reflected on windows. "You're almost out of time, Manny. Let's get out of here." Conner had no desire to explain himself to the sheriff. This looked bad no matter how it was viewed. Though he was on camera attempting to defuse the situation, that wouldn't mean much when everyone knew he'd been working with Manny just yesterday.

Multiple cars pulled up around them, boxing them in. Deputies gave orders for the crowd to disperse. The face-off was probably the most excitement these small-town folks had seen in weeks, while Conner was seriously ready for a vacation. Maybe if he got this done fast enough, he could get on that detail going with the president to Hawaii in a few months. He could probably persuade Kayla to come, too.

"Put the gun down, Manny. This doesn't have to end badly."

The man sneered. "You even sound like a

cop. *Put the gun down*," he mocked. "You only care about collateral, like I won't spray buckshot into this entire crowd. I shot you yesterday."

"I know. I have the bruise under my vest to prove it."

"Only a coward wears a vest, Thorne. You're nothing but a—" His voice descended into insults. "Next time I see you, you'll give me the girl and then I'll kill you. Andis can forget his grand plan."

Andis had a different plan? Conner wouldn't mind knowing more about that, but instead he said, "You won't see me again if I can help it. And you won't get your hands on Kayla."

As soon as he explained a couple of things to the sheriff, Conner was going to get out of here and get back to making sure she was okay.

The sheriff pulled up, along with two other county vehicles. In the pharmacy window's reflection, Conner could see the sheriff get out of his vehicle, one hand on the weapon on his hip. As the deputies and the sheriff walked over, guns now drawn, Conner glanced up at the window of Kayla's office. He couldn't see her, but he knew she was waiting for him.

"Guns down, gentlemen." The sheriff's methodology was so passive Conner had long figured it would get him in trouble. The man relied on the respect he'd earned after years of service to sway people. Which was fine with those who genuinely appreciated what he did. The rest of the county's citizens didn't care what he ordered them to do.

Conner shifted his grip so his finger was nowhere near the trigger and turned his gun sideways. He waited for Manny to begin to crouch and lowered himself in sync with the man. "Sheriff, if I could have a—"

A deputy grabbed Conner's hands and pulled them behind his back. Another did the same with Manny while the sheriff made his way to the pharmacist.

"Both of you can say what you have to say at my office."

What? He couldn't get hauled in. He had to get back to Kayla. To make sure she was safe. "But I—"

Manny shot a dirty look at Conner.

"They were going to kill me," the pharmacist yelled.

He turned to the old man, who still had both hands raised. Beyond him, the crowd had drifted away. No one was there. "Kayla's hiding, and I need to make sure she's—"

The sheriff grabbed his arm. "Conner Thorne, you're under arrest."

* * *

Kayla watched the man duck into the kitchen. The phone pressed against her ear was warm now. "Yes, he went in."

"Then go. Run, Kayla."

Who'd have thought the last number before she'd dialed the sheriff—labeled Mom in Conner's contacts—would turn out to be his handler. He'd said it, but she hadn't really believed it. She'd needed help, so she'd prayed and dialed. *Thank You, Lord.* He'd saved her again, His love for her overwhelming even when she was alone and in danger.

Now Greg's voice gave her the strength she needed to hold on to the laptop and the mental clarity to pray she didn't fall down the stairs. Her head still pounded from the crash the night before, and her body ached in ways she didn't want to think about, none of which were going to go away soon.

Her car was still trashed. That whole incident hit her all over again, and she had to force herself to think even as she turned and ran down the sidewalk toward Conner's truck. He'd left the keys in the visor—another blessing. She'd seen the sheriff haul him away and had told Greg.

"How are you doing?"

Right. He was still on the line. "Almost there."

"Good girl. We can get you to the team. You just have to get in the truck and you can meet them halfway."

The truck.

Kayla pumped her legs as hard as she could and sucked in breaths, but her diaphragm didn't want her to go that fast. Even if it was going to save her life.

She didn't know the man who'd been in her office. She'd never seen him before, but he was huge and not someone she wanted to be alone with. She wanted Conner, who'd been hauled away by the sheriff like some common criminal instead of the good man he was. So good. More noble than she could ever credit herself with being.

Kayla told her body to slow, but not quickly enough. She collided with the truck's driver's door with an "Oof."

Greg said, "Kayla, you okay?"

"Yep." She shifted the laptop in her arm and exhaled.

"I have all day, Kayla. I'm not going to let you off the phone."

Because he was Secret Service, and that was what he was paid for. Not that she wasn't grateful. Kayla respected the job the agents did and the raw deal they sometimes got when the president's schedule was packed out and they were rotated from detail to detail with hardly any breaks.

Kayla hauled the door open. It creaked all the way until it was wide enough for her to slip in, but she never made it.

The warmth of a person. A huge person. Came up right behind her. Close enough to touch.

"Give me the laptop."

EIGHT

The sheriff entered the interrogation room—the only one in this dinky small-town office—carrying a paper cup of coffee. He set it down on his side of the table and sat across from Conner. Like he hadn't kept Conner cuffed and waiting for an hour.

"All righty, let's get started, shall we?"

Conner had exhausted his patience. "How about you start with what you're charging me with."

The sheriff lifted one gray eyebrow. "That can wait, I think. We have things to talk about. Besides, from what I saw, Manny was the one with the beef and you were trying to protect innocents." He paused. "Which tells me I might be on the right track."

"If we're just talking, maybe I could call Kayla. Make sure she's safe."

The sheriff took a sip of his coffee. "She's

good. She's the one who called and told me about Manny, though I was already on my way there."

Conner exhaled. Hopefully, she was hanging tight in her office. She had his phone, and she knew who to call if she needed help. Still, all Conner wanted to do was get this over with so he could find Kayla and reassure himself that she was safe.

The sheriff set his cup down. He hadn't brought a file in with him, but he still might have looked up Conner's name. He'd have found only what the Secret Service planted on Conner's record. A couple of fake misdemeanors that showed a penchant toward being a hothead. When added to his Secret Service record, they made him look unpredictable, like a loose cannon.

"Now, you feel like telling me what the bad blood is between you and Manny Santee?"

"He wants to kill me," Conner said. "He also wants to kill Kayla. But I thought we weren't going to talk about what just happened."

The sheriff didn't answer the question. "And why would he want that?"

"Orders."

"From Andis?"

Conner shrugged. "He didn't really take the time to explain while he was burning down

Kayla's office, running us off the road with his truck and threatening to kill the pharmacist."

The sheriff's eyebrows rose. "So press charges. I can only do so much with what I have from the fire and what I saw today on the street. My dispatcher didn't show up for work today and no one's seen her. I need your statements if I'm going to make a case stick."

"Kayla was planning to come see you today. If you let me call her, I can get her here and she can make her statement."

"Funny, you don't talk like a common thug."

"Regardless of what I do for a living now, you don't get to be a Secret Service agent by being dumb."

The older man frowned. "No, I don't suppose you do."

"And working for Andis Bamir doesn't make me heartless. As much as he might want me to be."

The sheriff's attention stilled. "Which makes me wonder, guy like you, smart as you are, why would you be hanging out with Andis Bamir? Rolling with his guys, leaning on townspeople so they live in fear of the next time they see Manny's truck drive down the street."

"If he's the threat, why am I here? You should be talking to him, shouldn't you?"

"You tell me." The sheriff took another healthy sip of coffee. "Mmm. That's good stuff."

Conner could have rolled his eyes. Was the guy trying to make him crack and spill everything he knew just because he was thirsty?

When he didn't say anything, the sheriff shrugged. "So Manny's trying to kill both of you because Andis ordered him to, or maybe for another reason. Here's what I think." The older man paused for dramatic effect. If Conner wasn't so preoccupied worrying about Kayla, he'd have laughed. "I think there might be a reason why you're here, working for Andis. A reason that might be more than money or the chance to do something illegal for the rush of it. I don't doubt this is a job—I'm just wondering precisely what kind of job it is."

Okay, so he was reaching for Conner to tell him that he was undercover Secret Service here to bring down Andis. Like he'd actually come out and say that. Manny and Andis distrusting and suspecting him now was one thing. Telling the sheriff voluntarily was entirely something else. There was no way Conner would give this man the satisfaction of letting him know he guessed right while Conner was sitting here cuffed and Kayla was still very much in danger.

The sheriff stared. "Not going to answer?"

This man might be a "good" guy, but Conner wasn't going to break cover. It was just so ingrained in him not to, whether word was out or not. The sheriff could be asking for Andis, or he could be asking completely innocently. Conner had no way to tell, and he didn't know the sheriff well enough to figure it out. There was no reason for this man to know why Conner was in town or that he worked undercover for the Secret Service. He'd lie to protect the integrity of the job, and he'd definitely lie to protect Kayla.

"Not saying anything is, in effect, speaking." The sheriff paused again for a swig of his coffee. "So here's the thing. The reason I'm talking to you and not to Manny. Yet. Tell me, what would you say to a…partnership of sorts? Not officially, you understand. I can't put any of this on record. But I feel like we could help each other out."

Conner leaned back in his chair. The man wanted to team up? Conner had burned whatever trust he'd worked at with Andis. The man wanted him taken down, and Manny was the weapon he would use to carry out that sentence. Whatever the sheriff had planned, he doubted it would work. He had no credibility now, not with anyone except Greg.

They needed to get this over with so Conner could go find Kayla. For the sake of moving things along, he said, "Tell me what you want me to do." As long as the sheriff thought he was interested, he wouldn't charge Conner with anything.

Conner had never been tempted to pray before, but he was now. He knew Kayla had faith in God and that God didn't always do what she thought He should, but she said she trusted that He knew what was best regardless.

Keep her safe.

He figured God had a vested interest in someone who followed Him. He wouldn't let her come to harm. And if the sheriff wanted to talk, that was fine. This was a chance to find out where this guy was at.

"Well, it goes like this," the sheriff said. "All you'd need to do is shoot me a text when Andis is headed somewhere. Let me know when he's off to make a deal or what he's working on. Maybe take a photo of someone he meets with and pass me the picture. Shouldn't be too hard. Not for a man with your…training. It would help me out a lot, especially if you see him hanging around a certain property. The old paper mill out west of town."

"It's abandoned now, isn't it? They closed it down." That was common knowledge in town. As were the two murders that had taken place there years ago.

"I'd like to know if Andis is ever there."

Conner shrugged like there was nothing special about that property. He'd figured Andis used the mill to get the distinct paper he needed to print counterfeit money, but he'd never found any evidence of recent activity. It was like no new money had been printed in months, for some reason. If the sheriff suspected Andis was conducting business there, then it could be that Andis had simply relocated his operation.

Regardless of whether Conner was a Secret Service agent or not, the sheriff was playing a dangerous game. He wanted Conner to *spy* on Andis for him, like some kind of double agent? The man had just handed Conner his safety, and his career, on a platter.

Kayla struggled. Fire burned in her arms as she gripped the laptop for dear life.

"Give it to me," the man grunted.

"No!"

Kayla stomped for his shoe, missed and caught his shin. The man cried out as her heel glanced off the front of his leg. He called her a foul name, but Kayla didn't let it bother her. She jabbed two fingers at his eyes. He let go and she grabbed the door handle.

She pulled the door open and moved to get

in but her body was hauled back by two meaty hands. Kayla swung at him with the laptop.

Conner sat up straight. Since the fire at Kayla's office he'd blown his cover. Andis had probably put it together that he was still Secret Service—though no one would officially confirm it either way.

He said, "If I go straight to Andis and tell him what you asked me to do, what do you think will happen? I could trade you to get my position back, and you're hosed. Done. Dead, probably."

The sheriff coughed. "Yes, I would imagine my life somewhat short-lived after that."

"Because he'd send Manny to put a bullet in you. The way he tried to do with me." Conner could only hope the sheriff wouldn't get killed the way he and Kayla almost had.

The sheriff said, "There are risks and I understand that. What I need you to understand is that the people of this town can't live much longer under the thumb of a criminal. A thug."

"You want to go up against him?"

The sheriff's face contorted. "Andis Bamir will pay for what he's doing to this town." His face reddened. He balled his fist and slammed it on the table. "He'll pay!"

"Because you're going to kill him?"

"I'm going to bring him down." The sheriff

lifted his hand in a fist and punched the air with the force of a tossed balloon.

Conner got up. This man wanted to start a war with Conner—and Kayla—in the middle? They were already in the fight of their lives.

"Sit down, Agent Thorne."

Conner turned but didn't sit. If Sheriff Johnson wanted him to keep listening, the man was going to have to bring charges against him. There wasn't much the sheriff could say that would induce Conner to make a deal that put Kayla's life in even more danger.

Conner said, "A man like you, I figure you have your hand on the pulse of what's going on in this town. You'll understand why I had to work twice as hard to make sure Andis trusted me. Manny never did. Not with my history as an agent. It was only because of the intel I could give them that they let me in at all."

The sheriff huffed.

"So tell me," Conner said. There had to be something. The sheriff's reaction wasn't just about a crime wave, not when he'd gotten that emotional. "What is between you and Andis?"

"Aside from me being the law in this county and his breaking it?"

Conner shrugged one shoulder.

"It was back when Andis first came to this town. Those two murders at the mill had gone cold, and I knew I'd never figure it out. Then Andis showed up." Sheriff Johnson sighed. "Saw him for what he was right away. But what was I going to do? Surveillance, sure. But I'm no covert agent, so Andis knew I was watching for him to trip up. Turns out it was me who would trip.

"Someone leaked to the paper that I was involved in a scam a local real estate agent was running. Paying off the building inspector. They made it look like I got payoffs, as well, when I assure you that I did not. There are no skeletons in this closet."

If that was true, Conner figured the sheriff was the only person on earth who could say that. Everyone had something about themselves that they didn't want anyone to know.

The sheriff continued, "My name was discredited anyway, even with no evidence but what they'd made up. Nearly lost my job. My wife packed and went to her sister's in the next county. By the time I managed to prove my innocence, the damage had been done. She filed for divorce and started dating the sheriff over there. His daughter's kids call her Gramma."

The sheriff sighed. "So I kept digging, found enough I could get a warrant to arrest him for harassment, intimidation. A little theft and some forgery, considering he bought that house under a fake name. Nothing big, but enough I was an annoyance he couldn't ignore."

Conner nodded.

"He's left me alone since. Operates on the edges of the county, and I know he leans on the business owners. But I can't get proof. No one will talk, and if anyone has reported it, someone buried the file or never entered it as a case. I haven't seen it. And if my dispatcher is involved, I'll figure it out. When I find her."

Could be he had a deputy sympathetic to Andis, as well. Conner wouldn't be surprised if that was the case. Andis enjoyed the power of having people on all sides of the law under his thumb.

"He was supposed to lie low, keep things on the outskirts of town. Run his business in a way it doesn't creep inward to the people here. Instead he has spread right to Main Street like a poison. Andis Bamir has not been keeping up his end of our agreement, and it's time I stop playing by the rules before he infects this whole town." The sheriff shrugged. "You of all people know what he's capable of. That's why I think it's you who can help me."

Kayla had put it together, and she was a smart woman, so it hadn't been hard for her. It was his experience that people saw what they wanted to see, and they believed what they wanted to believe. The sheriff wanted him to confirm what he thought.

"Counterfeit money, right?" Conner didn't give him anything. The man sighed. "Secret Service. Counterfeit money. It's not that much of a stretch, and they did a good job making you look like a turncoat. Betraying the oath you swore, giving away their secrets to make money no matter what laws you broke or who got hurt."

Accepting that it was easier—and quicker—to confirm and explain why he couldn't help, Conner said, "I can't help you get concrete evidence on Andis. If I get anything, I turn it over to the people I report to. This is bigger than your county, and I'm way past surveillance. I was in tight with them. Now I've got next to nothing. The mill is a dead end, and Andis didn't give me anything but to flash superbills in my face."

"Superbills?"

"Expert forgeries. Now they're not going to trust me trying to fish for info. Not any more than they let me in on what that was with Kayla or why their operation suddenly stopped."

The sheriff said, "They will if I tell Manny I'm letting him go to get in with Andis. I'll tell them you're Secret Service to buy myself a way onto their team. It'll take some explaining and you can help me work up a story, but I'll be able to operate from the inside. Convince them

I know how to get *you*. Then you come in from the other side and hit them. Misdirection. They won't know which of us is on what side, who is with them and who isn't."

Conner thought about it. He could use an ally, but they weren't going to be partners. Kayla had been on her own long enough already, and it was time for him to go.

He stood up. "I'll keep your offer in mind. I'll even run it by my handler, see what we think might be the best way forward."

"You aren't going to help me."

"I'm going to help Kayla Harris. If I can bring Andis down in the meantime, fine." He gave the sheriff Greg's number. "Call him yourself and talk about it." Conner wasn't going to admit out loud that since he'd run into Kayla, every priority he'd had changed. He was barely prepared to admit it to himself.

She was everything. She always had been, and seeing her again only cemented the fact that she always would be.

The sheriff set his phone on the table and dialed the number. "Hang out for a second." It rang through the speaker.

"Conner? Is that you?" Greg sounded out of breath.

"I'm here, but it's Sheriff Johnson who wants to talk to you."

"And Kayla?"

"She's not here."

Greg told him she'd been on the phone with him. That he'd heard a man's voice and then she had screamed. Conner's insides froze. "So where is she now?"

A door crashed open, out in the main office area. "I need help!"

Conner left the phone on the table and ran out of the room. Kayla stood at the door, blood on her forehead coming from a wicked knot on her temple.

"Kayla," he breathed, and ran over to her. She fell into his arms like she was made to be there. "Are you okay?"

"I am now."

Conner smiled back at her. Before he realized he was doing it, his mouth was halfway to her lips. Just a simple touch. It would be so easy. So natural for them to—

The sheriff cleared his throat. "Ms. Harris. Let's get you a doctor. Do you need to sit down?"

She flushed and Conner could have kicked himself, letting her stand when she should be sitting. She was injured and he was thinking about kissing her? What was wrong with him?

She glanced at him before she told the sheriff, "I'm okay, other than my head." She looked back at Conner. "My laptop was stolen."

NINE

"Are you sure you're okay?"

Kayla nodded. The concern in Conner's eyes was enough to clear the cloud of pain from her head. No doubt it'd be a roaring headache later, but for now all she could think about was the fact that he'd been about to kiss her. Kiss her!

For just a second, the stress and fear of the past two days had dissipated. All that had mattered to her was him and the look in his eyes—the one that was still there. She wanted to wrap herself up in his arms, shut her eyes tight and block out the world.

"What happened?"

Kayla didn't want to talk about it, but they had to know. "It was a man. I've never seen him before—I don't know who he was." She told the sheriff about his clothing and his hair. The impression she'd gotten of his face was like a bulldog.

Sheriff Johnson nodded and made notes on a pad.

Kayla tried to think it through. "He came up behind me outside. Grabbed me. I fought him off, tried to get in the car, but he caught me." Breath hitched in her throat. "He slammed me against the truck."

Conner's hand settled on her shoulder, but he didn't say anything.

"I must have blacked out for a second, or I just couldn't think because I was dazed, because then I was alone and the laptop was gone. I don't think he opened the lid, or he'd have seen the keyboard suffered damage in the fire." With a wry smile, she reached up and touched Conner's hand with hers, just to hold on to. "I drove straight here."

The sheriff said, "Do you think you could look at mug shots, see if you recognize any of them?"

She nodded. "I can certainly try." Kayla wanted to smile but couldn't muster up much gumption. She hadn't been this tired before lunch in so long. How would she make it through the rest of the day?

"Kayla's wiped. Maybe I could bring her back later?"

The sheriff shrugged. "Sooner would be better. I also have to figure out what to do with

Manny Santee. I could charge him, and the pharmacist already made his statement." He left it open, inviting discussion.

Kayla looked at Conner, trying to figure out why it seemed like the sheriff was asking him permission to formally detain someone. Were they working together now? Conner nodded, though it was a little sardonic. He didn't want to work with the man. Probably more because he wasn't a team player than just because it was Sheriff Johnson. Conner had worked alone so long she wondered over the fact that he'd let her in at all. But he seemed to soak up having her there.

Had he gone so long without a friend that he'd needed someone, or was it that it was *her*? Kayla knew which she would prefer. The idea that he had feelings for her made her heart soar. She didn't want to be just another protectee. Just another person to put his life on the line for.

Noble, but the idea of him dying made her want to cry. Maybe it was just that she was tired, or that she'd had a crazy couple of days and nearly died more than once. But no matter how Conner had intended to come off so many times, Kayla couldn't stop the movie reel in her head. The action shot where Conner, dressed in his Secret Service suit with the earpiece and sunglasses, did that sacrifice-all hero dive in front of her and took the bullet.

He would do it. Of *course* he would do it. Conner would take the bullet. He'd give his life for her and she would be left here to live the rest of her life without him. Like that was any consolation. Being alive, trying to be happy or function like a normal person without him.

The noise that came from her throat sounded like a growl.

"Kayla, you okay?" Like he was completely innocent.

Thankfully, the sheriff was across the room getting them both coffee. She could use a jolt of java.

"I don't want to leave. I want to look at the mug shots." She didn't want to talk about the Secret Service oath he'd taken. As though her life was more important than his. No way. He'd totally sacrifice himself for her. But it would be for duty, not love. Instead, what she wanted was him here with her, as well as the love.

Because, truthfully, Kayla had probably been in love with him for years. Though for a long time it had been a childish crush. Now those feelings were growing. Could she trust them? Could she trust Conner with them, or would he disregard her the way he had years ago? She wanted to believe he would have a care with her feelings, but the reality was that she just didn't know.

She would guard her heart, because she wanted to find out.

"Here you go, Ms. Harris."

"Thank you." She took the disposable cup from Sheriff Johnson and pulled her chair up to the computer. He opened a database and she was able to narrow down ethnicity and age range. Hopefully, the man was local. And had been arrested before.

Conner tried not to stare at the back of her head like a weirdo. Something was going on in Kayla's mind and he had no idea what it was. Too bad he couldn't just ask her. Right now he had to find out what the sheriff was planning on doing with Manny.

"Sheriff?" When the older man turned, Conner said, "You mentioned letting Manny go. What would be your plan?" He had to have one. Why else would the sheriff let Manny leave without charging him? The object wasn't to let him get away with threatening the pharmacist, but to catch Andis and bring down the whole operation.

"He's close to Andis. Keeping tabs on him could get us intel."

Like Conner hadn't been doing that for

months. Really, they needed a warrant to run surveillance on Manny, but this was about keeping Kayla safe. "If we can get a bug on him, or at least a tracker on his phone, we can stay one step ahead. We'll know where he's going and what he's there for. That would definitely give us an edge. Soon as there's a Secret Service team in town for support, we can get agents on Manny. See what they come up with."

"If your team could get us a bug, I can plant it on Manny when I let him go."

Conner wasn't certain how good the man would be at making that smooth, but he was willing to let it play out and see what happened. Manny was going to be suspicious if the sheriff didn't sell it right. He'd be wary at suddenly being let go. Would the team get here in time? "What are you going to tell him?"

"That I made a deal with Andis, that he called and told me to let Manny go. I'll call Andis and spin the same tale. I can play the part of oppressed, downtrodden, ineffective sheriff pretty well. They'll buy it because neither of them think much of me."

Conner shrugged. It could be enough. "Just as long as he's far away from Kayla, I don't care what he believes."

She was still going through mug shots, scanning pictures as she sipped that awful coffee.

He probably needed to get a doctor to see her. If she'd hit her head when she was slammed against the truck the way she had when Manny ran them off the road, she might be injured worse now. He didn't need her to end up with a medical emergency because they hadn't been cautious enough with her health.

He'd had a friend in the Secret Service who'd been hit on the head and thought he was fine. Later he'd been hospitalized. He'd needed surgery because he had a bleed in his brain. It was the last thing he wanted for Kayla.

"I'll call the team," he said. "See what we can do about getting Manny GPS tracked."

"GP—" Kayla turned. "My laptop has that. It has software that lets you track its location. We just have to turn the software on—then when they switch my computer on and connect to the internet, we'll know where it is." She paused. "Assuming they can do that when it suffered so much damage. Does Andis have a techy person on his payroll?"

"Yes," Conner said. "There are tech people on his payroll, and he has access to some pretty slick technology."

If the GPS was on when it was connected, that meant they could get her computer back. Hopefully before whoever stole it got into the system and Kayla's emails. A woman and child were out there relying on people they didn't know to keep them safe. Conner wasn't going to be the one who let them down, and he was proud of Kayla for fighting her attacker the best she could. She had nothing to feel bad for.

"The computer store might help Andis, but they'll help me, too." She picked up the desk phone, a determined look on her face. "I have to call Drew. Get him to turn it on."

Her smile lifted some of the weight from Conner's shoulders. Sure, he shouldn't be burdened by her state of mind, but could he help it if he wanted to see her happy instead of just resolute and focused? He couldn't stand to see any more of that fear on her face.

Conner was going to do whatever he could to keep her happy, even if that meant letting her go so she could find that man she was looking for—the one who didn't know anything about her past. As if someone who didn't understand her could hope to have a shot at making her happy for the rest of her life.

This was a small town. He could be content living in a place like this, but not this town. He needed somewhere people didn't know him as Andis's associate. Kayla could come with him. They could pack their bags and just drive, find some Midwestern town where people said hi to each other on the street. He could find simple work and put a ring on her finger. Be the man who got to protect her every day for the rest of her life.

The years had made him surer than ever that they were made for each other. Everything about Kayla felt right, whether or not he fought against the idea. Whether or not it was cool to start a relationship now, when it never had been before. He wanted that dream with her—the one his parents had shown him, up until his father's problems came to light. She was everything he'd ever wanted.

And...when did he turn into a sap?

One minute he was thinking about her with someone else, and the next he was thinking about a little girl with her pouty lips asking for a pony.

Conner had to focus.

"Thanks, Drew." She hung up.

"All good?"

Kayla nodded. "He's going to log in to the website and switch the GPS software on."

Conner said, "So who is this Drew guy anyway?" Okay, so now he sounded totally jealous.

Kayla's look said she'd heard it in his voice, too. "Drew is twenty and runs the computer store. He sold me my phone and he set up my computer for me when I moved into my office in town. He's basically my technical support, and we figured out we share a love of alien movies. So we went to a new release one time." She shrugged. "I don't want him to be helping Andis, but I don't want his life to be in danger either."

Conner nodded. "Did you find anything in the pictures?"

"Actually, I might have." She pointed to the screen. "That one."

The sheriff's eyebrows lifted. Conner said, "Someone you know?"

"Actually," the sheriff answered, "that's interesting if it was the person who took the computer. Is that who you saw, Kayla?"

She frowned, her eyes on the screen. "I *think* so, but I'm not sure. Who is he?"

The sheriff clicked and brought up his name and a list of charges, including forgery and Social Security fraud. "His name is Tim Harmer. He's Jan Barton's boyfriend."

Conner stood with Kayla in the interrogation room while the sheriff brought Manny out. She stood still and quiet, watching the doorway. Conner glanced back for a second and then whispered, "Why don't you sit—"

She lifted a finger to her lips. "Shh."

Conner pressed his lips together.

"Let's go out the back way. Less people." The sheriff's voice drifted to them.

"Just so long as I get out of here, I don't much care what arrangement you made with Andis," Manny said. "It's your deal, and believe me, he'll make you pay."

The sheriff's voice turned emotional as he explained something about a problem he was having. Conner couldn't make out most of it, but the man sold it well. Hopefully, Manny bought it.

"What about Thorne?"

The sheriff's voice was audible when he said, "The other guy? Conner?"

"That's the one. You let him go, too?" He almost sounded like there was no ulterior motive for asking the question. Almost.

"Figured I owed the guy a head start." The sheriff chuckled. "This cat-and-mouse thing you've got going with him is cute and all, but I can't have any more townspeople getting caught in the cross fire. Do you know how much grief I'm going to get from the pharmacist after that stunt you pulled in the street?"

Sheriff Johnson continued, "No. I'm not letting him go until you're out of here. And don't think about hanging around outside either, waiting for him. You gotta be long gone before he shows his face. Go ask your boss what the plan is."

Conner figured that would work in the short term, but soon enough Manny would figure out that he and Andis had been played and come gunning for the sheriff. The Secret Service would protect him, though. The team would be broken apart to cover Kayla, Sheriff Johnson, Andis and his men, and Conner, but they'd get better results that way. More chances to land on something solid and cover everything—everyone—they needed to.

Kayla's fingers touched his hand and he realized he'd balled his fist tight. Conner unfurled his hand and took hers with a smile. Everything would work out—he'd make sure of that. As long as she believed it, that was what mattered. She had to know he would make everything good for her.

"Whatever," Manny said. "I'm out of here."

The voices faded.

"Kayla?" Conner kept his voice quiet, just in case someone could hear. "You okay?"

She shut her eyes for a second, dark circles there. She'd never looked more delicate or in need of him to… He didn't know. Hug her?

Conner gathered her into his arms and she tilted up her face. Kayla moved her mouth up toward his and her eyes drifted closed. She thought he was going to kiss her?

Conner wanted to, sure. But this wasn't the

time. Wasn't she worried about the timing? Before he left her hanging, Conner touched her cheek with his and hugged her with their faces side by side. Her hair touched his nose and he felt the intake of breath when she probably realized he wasn't going to kiss her. Conner rubbed her shoulders and gave her a squeeze like he didn't notice.

"Kayla— Oh." The sheriff cleared his throat. "Drew called back. He's on the line for you."

Conner let her go. Kayla scooted past the sheriff and out of the room without looking at him. She had nothing to be embarrassed about, not as far as he could see. But she was.

Conner touched the bridge of his nose and then followed her out of the interrogation room. One day he'd figure out how to do this without upsetting her. At least, he hoped he could.

"Okay, thanks. I owe you. Now stay safe, and don't go to work today. Okay? Good." She hung up and turned to the computer, opened the browser and typed in an address.

"Where is it?"

"That's what I'm finding out." She didn't turn around. The map loaded, and Conner leaned in. "Do you know where that is?"

He nodded, his chin almost touching her shoulder. "I do." Conner straightened and she turned, looked at him. The embarrassment had gone, or she'd chosen to set it aside for the time being. Later he could tell her how badly he'd wanted to kiss her. "That's a construction site."

"Why would my laptop be at a construction site? Do they even have Wi-Fi for it to connect to?"

He shrugged. "They're building an apartment complex. And not well. The owner owes Andis a lot of money, so he's breathing down the guy's neck until he pays up or Andis can extract what he's owed. He'd have me hang out at the site, make sure the guy showed up every day and track him down if he didn't. It was basically babysitting, watching the man cut corners every which way."

"And now my computer was taken there. By Jan Barton's boyfriend." She said it like she hardly believed everything that was happening.

"Does he work for Andis?" The sheriff's question brought Conner's head around.

He thought it over for a second. "What were the charges on the boyfriend's convictions?"

The sheriff read them off.

Conner could have kicked himself. "Andis doesn't make the money. He hires it out." Conner pointed to the mug shot. "To this guy. Tim Harmer. Everything about that history says counterfeiter."

Kayla said, "So why is Tim Harmer after

my computer? To try to find Andis's wife and daughter, or to find Jan? Or is it some other reason?"

"That's a great question."

One Conner had no idea the answer to.

TEN

Conner drove with one hand and gripped the phone with the other while he listened to Locke. His former team leader was now a director, and not happy at all that he hadn't been read in to what Conner's new job was. When Greg had asked for a detail, the request had passed up the chain high enough that Locke realized what was happening. In true Locke fashion, that meant he was heading up the team on its way to town.

"Should be there in half an hour."

Conner gave him the address to the construction site. "When we get there, we'll wait for you. I don't want Kayla outside of protection." The team could watch her while he and Locke found the computer.

He hung up. Conner was so scared she was going to get seriously hurt that he was almost ready to tell them to take her in—okay...*detain her.* And he would do it. She'd be alive, out of Andis's reach in protective custody. Sure, she'd probably hate him for doing it, but she'd forgive him.

He'd seen evidence of faith in her life, at her house. The Bible in her purse. Scriptures scribbled on three-by-five cards she'd had hung on her fridge. God wasn't someone he'd thought about since he was a kid. His mom had taken him to church every Sunday, but with college and then the start of his career, Conner hadn't had much time or the inclination to keep up with it.

Now they just had to stay far enough under Andis's radar and out of Manny's reach long enough to uncover the source of the counterfeit money, the superbills. Not that the Secret Service wanted to admit there were stellar forgeries floating around, but it was what it was.

The only way he'd accept her having been in danger was if he fully completed this case. Lesser charges weren't part of his plan. Conner wanted the whole operation brought down. Kayla had been hurt enough. He didn't like the fact that Kayla was part of it, but if she was close to him, he could at least make sure she stayed safe. Otherwise he'd be so distracted he'd just worry the whole time. And if they got a win? It might actually be worth it.

"You're quiet. I don't think that's a good thing."

Conner smiled but didn't glance over at her. "Have you prayed?"

"I haven't stopped praying since you walked into my office."

"My mom used to do that. Every single time, she'd grab my hand and close her eyes. I'd just stand there until she said, 'Amen.'"

"She didn't say the words out loud?"

"Nope." He shook his head, the smile still on his lips. "Mostly I figure she didn't want me to hear what she was saying to Him about me."

Kayla giggled. "Interesting."

Conner laughed. "It was effective, I'll tell you. Who knew what she was asking? Or what she was telling God about me. I'd behave myself each time after. For at least a day."

Kayla laughed. The sound made his heart catch, but he couldn't let it distract him. Conner had to concentrate, especially considering they weren't going on the run. No, they were going right back into the lion's den.

Undercover work had taken all the dark parts of Conner and brought them to the surface. He couldn't let Kayla see more of that darkness. Conner was no hero; he was just a guy trying to do his job.

He blew out a breath and fought to gain control as they got closer to the construction site.

He couldn't go there like this. He'd blow it and Locke would know just how close to the edge he was.

Kayla really had no clue how thrown he was by the idea of her being in danger. There was something about her that he couldn't shake. She had to be safe, or he'd be no good.

How he'd thought he would find peace with a woman like Kayla was anyone's guess. Conner knew what he wanted, but the jury was still out on whether it was best for her. She probably didn't need some hothead in her life, dictating security measures. He'd go too far, and she would have to put space between them because he'd let his fear get the better of him.

"How is it going to go with Locke?"

Conner winced at her question.

"I'm serious. He flipped out on the phone, right?" When he nodded, she said, "How can he not have known?"

Conner clicked on his blinker and took the turn before he answered. "It's need to know, and Locke didn't. The fewer people who know the real story behind my being 'fired' from the Secret Service, the better. Andis checked up on me. We couldn't hide the fact that I was Secret Service. That was public knowledge. But we could spin it."

"So they all think you betrayed the service. That you're a bad guy."

"That's the point, Kayla. It had to be believable, or Andis would never have bought it. I was ready for a change and thinking about quitting. But I was never sure I wanted to give up the Secret Service. A week later I got an offer to transfer and go undercover."

"That scares me."

He pulled up at the stoplight and turned to her. "What scares you?"

"You do. You've convinced everyone you're a bad guy. You walk around all day pretending to be a bad guy. Don't you worry you'll start to believe it's true?"

The light turned green and he set off. She'd voiced the very worry he had in his report. Not the official report, but the one he had to submit to the shrink. Half the time he couldn't remember any more if the real Conner Thorne was a good guy or a bad guy.

"What do you think I am?" Maybe he didn't want to know the answer, but the question was out already. Conner had to accept her honesty. She'd give him no less than that.

"You've always had an edge, ever since I've known you. There's something wild and dangerous in you, Conner Thorne. Something that is really, really bad for me."

Maybe she should pack a bag and get out of town if she thought that. He could clear this up and be gone before she got back.

"And yet I can't seem to bring myself to leave. Not now that you're here." She twisted in her seat. "There's something about you. Something I never once forgot."

Conner nodded. That was so true. He felt the exact same way about her, to the point he'd stayed away for months when he found out she lived here. It was only because he'd heard Andis and Manny say her name that he'd made contact. If they hadn't, Conner would not have shown up in her office the night before. He'd have stayed away, and she'd never have known he was there.

Kayla went on. "Locke knows that, deep down, you're a good guy."

Conner wasn't so sure. And he didn't want to talk about Locke. "Did the motel call back about Jan Barton yet?"

She shook her head. "The sheriff should be there by now."

"So, what? You take the women to the motel and they have to make their own way to the ranch?"

"No," Kayla answered. "I have the house manager come and get them. It's safer for me to be separate from it. Locke explains it better than I do. But I have to be one step removed. It keeps my involvement to a minimum. And it was the only way he'd let me set it up."

Conner wanted to smile. At least someone had been looking out for her, even if it did have to be Locke. The man thought Kayla was the little sister he never had. "When the sheriff calls, we'll know for sure. He can ask Jan why her boyfriend wanted your computer."

Kayla nodded to the window. Fifteen minutes later he turned onto the street where the construction site was located. Conner glanced at her.

She shrugged. "What?"

"I don't want anyone to see you."

"Who came up with this plan?" Kayla muttered the question as she huddled down on the floor of the car in the backseat. Right. Like anyone who looked in the back window wouldn't see her crouched down there. But they were counting on everyone being occupied with their jobs, or if they weren't that they wouldn't care enough to check for a possible stowaway.

"Heads up." They turned the corner and drove for a minute. Then Conner stopped the car. "Huh."

Kayla readied herself. "What is it?"

"There's no one here. The whole place is deserted."

"Is that normal?"

"No. The owner is building an apartment complex that's like a collection of hipster townhomes. They've been rushing to get it done fast. Probably laundering Andis's counterfeit money through the operation, as well, to clean it up so his cash looks more legit."

Kayla lifted her head and looked around. Building frames, heavy equipment in the rutted dirt and a trailer that was probably the office.

Conner's chuckle shook the seat she was pressed against. "I've been alone for so long on this that…well, it's just really nice to have someone to talk to. You know?"

Kayla nodded before she realized he couldn't see her. "I know what you mean." Her independence wasn't in question, but forging her own path had left her with clients and not many friends. Before Conner showed up, she wouldn't have called herself lonely, but now she knew the feeling for what it really was. All those evenings with nothing to do. Weekends with no big plans.

Kayla halted her thoughts before they went too far. She had to stop categorizing her life as time spent "with Conner" and time "without

Conner." It had to just be her life, no matter whether he was there or not.

She sighed.

"You okay?"

"No one's here. How long will Locke be?" She leaned forward to see him look at his phone.

He sent a text to Locke and got a reply in seconds.

A truck hit a car on the highway. Stuck in traffic.

"So we just sit here?" Kayla glanced around. "The GPS said the laptop was here, and there's no one around. It won't hurt to look. I could grab it, and we can be on our way. That's better than just sitting here."

Conner turned enough so she could see the look in his eyes. That hard business look she recognized from years ago. "Hold."

She didn't smile until he got out. Studied the area, drew his weapon. It took a couple of minutes. Then he opened the door for her. He didn't look at her when she climbed out; he was scanning their surroundings. When they set off, it was because he indicated to her that they were ready to move. The whole thing washed back over her like muscle memory. Being protected. Her single-man security detail. Yes, please.

She didn't want that from anyone else, just him. Just as long as he was doing it because he was willing to admit he cared for her, not because of duty. Head down, she strode to the wood steps and up to the office. *God, please don't let there be anyone inside.* She stood back while Conner looked inside. He nodded to her— "Make it quick"—and then turned to guard the door while she went inside.

Kayla passed him, but she didn't pass up the opportunity to lean up on her tiptoes and kiss his cheek.

Then she ducked inside.

Kayla said a quick prayer she'd find the laptop and crossed to the desk. If it was here, it wasn't in plain view. Covered in papers, the desktop computer's keyboard had to be unearthed. She scanned the pages as she moved them aside. Invoices, lists of employee names and receipts. She jiggled the mouse and the monitor flicked on. The last person to use this computer had evidently not understood the clear line between work equipment and personal use, because while they'd logged off their social media account, the website was still open.

That, along with a program that would have interfaced with her laptop. Sure enough, a cord on top of the desk was the kind used to connect the two computers.

They'd accessed her laptop, but where was it?

Whoever worked in here seriously needed a

secretary. More papers and invoices filled the file cabinet, though not in any semblance of order. Was there a safe?

When she found an inspection report, Kayla stopped. Three different things concerning the electrics had been flagged. She had no idea what they were or what the implications were of their not being up to code, but someone had scribbled over the bottom half. Payment had been made. Kayla folded the paper, stuffed it in her back pocket and kept rifling through the file cabinet. If she couldn't find the laptop, maybe she could find something else to help Conner with his case.

Kayla pulled on the bottom drawer. Stuck.

She'd have to find more evidence, fast, if she wanted to be done before someone came in. Conner had told her to keep it to a couple of minutes, but this would take time. There were a ton of loose papers in here. Before regret or worry could take hold, Kayla pushed aside the errant thoughts and kept searching. A bank statement. An email about a problem with a shower leaking.

There was plenty to look into, but could they tie it back to Andis? She needed to find someone who could trace the information she had back to a company registered to his name or a business known to be his. It was all about association. There was a connection; she just had to figure out how to find it in a way that would make it hold up in court.

And she would be there. When Conner ended this case, when he testified against Andis and the man was finally put away for his crimes, Kayla was going to be there to look the man who had tormented a woman and her child in the eye. When the sentence was brought down, she would figure out how to contact Sofija and Lena and let them know that he was in prison.

That they were free.

Outside, a car drove across the gravel. Conner ducked inside. "Time to go, Kayla."

"One second. I just have to—"

"Now." He disappeared outside again.

Kayla yanked the drawer one more time, and it came open. "My laptop!" She grabbed it and ran to the door. Time to get out of there.

But it wasn't Conner at the door.

It was Andis Bamir.

ELEVEN

Manny's grin said it all. Conner stared at him, even as he watched Andis's back inside the office over Manny's shoulder. He could barely see the boss's arm and his shirt. Conner started to move around Manny, but he took a half step to the side. "Andis wants to talk to her." Like that was a good reason for Conner to stay out of it.

As if.

Conner said what he needed to say with a look. He shoved Manny's shoulder and strode past him to the wooden steps. How Andis knew they were going to be there was anyone's guess. It had to be a coincidence. They were supposed to have stayed out of his way, and he showed up at the exact place they were? Sure, it was Andis's business, but Conner was the one who took care of this place for the boss. Had this whole "chasing the laptop" exercise been a trap?

The only other explanation was that they were somehow tracking either him or Kayla and hadn't even realized the laptop was here. Perhaps Andis was having him followed. Or tracking his phone. They could be doing the same with Kayla, through that camera in her office, or her phone. But that didn't explain why they needed the laptop.

Conner stepped inside. "Everything okay?"

Kayla's eyes locked with his, and then he saw the gun. "Andis." He said the name like it was any other day and he wanted to greet the man. Conner's stomach was in knots. He wanted to step between them. To pull Kayla behind his back and protect her with his body, the way he'd been trained to do.

"Conner, I have to thank you for bringing Ms. Harris to me."

Her wide eyes darted to him and back to Andis. Her hands were clenched at her sides, the muscles of her forearms taut. Her cheeks were flushed, but she held her shoulders as though she was ready to bolt at any moment.

And there was nothing Conner could do about it.

Andis went on, "I wouldn't have been so concerned about your loyalty if I'd known you would bring her to me this fast."

Kayla's face changed from a look of fear to one of betrayal. She couldn't believe this was his doing, could she? He would have thought there was no way she could think that. Conner gave her a quick shake of his head and then said, "Of course. Anything to clear up the confusion."

If he didn't agree, Andis would likely shoot him and the case would fall apart. After that, Kayla's body would turn up in the woods miles away, where it couldn't be traced back to Andis Bamir. They'd probably frame Conner for the murder after they made him "disappear," too.

"Though I don't think killing Kayla will help, not when you've already got the laptop," Conner said, as nonchalant as he could. "Too much heat when the body of former President Harris's daughter gets discovered by a hiker."

Andis said, "I have you to make sure the evidence doesn't lead anywhere. Don't I?" He motioned to Conner with his head and told Kayla, "Your boyfriend is good at disappearing bodies. Did he tell you that?"

It was true, in a way. He'd relocated eight people, two of them with their families, since he'd gone undercover. He'd told Andis they were dead, taken a couple of convincing photos using movie makeup and had Greg send them on to their new lives in some other state—or into witness protection.

A good thing, a right thing in the middle of this mess of gray areas. Right. Wrong. Conner was so far under he had trouble figuring out the difference anymore. Sure, he'd saved lives and not killed as Andis had ordered him, but that didn't really make him a good guy. He'd still done plenty of bad things for Andis.

Dread settled over her face. Conner cleared his throat. "How about we just get to the point?"

Kayla didn't belong here, not with a man like Andis, and not with him. She belonged in her girlie house with her pedigree and her fancy job. Sure, that wasn't exactly fair, but it was true. They didn't mix.

"Certainly." Andis's aim with the gun wasn't so determined, but Kayla didn't relax. He said, "I simply wish to know where my wife and daughter are. That is all."

"What makes you think I know where they are?" Her voice was small, her spirit broken. Conner felt the impact of it like a physical pain in his chest.

"You are responsible for their disappearance. Now, since you came all this way to retrieve your laptop, I suggest you use it to find them."

It *was* a setup. They'd been lured here, all because Andis needed Kayla to use the laptop to find his family. Of course.

She said, "Are you the one who put the surveillance system in my office?"

Andis's mouth twitched, but he didn't answer. Years ago she'd have fibbed her way out of the situation—and out of the consequences of her actions. This Kayla, the incredible woman she'd grown into, was strong and honorable. Which only made Conner all the more aware of the ways she had outgrown him. She'd flourished, and it was beautiful to see. But like looking at a rare book behind a glass case. No touching allowed.

And he'd brought her right to Andis.

The man didn't back down. "Did you somehow forget where you sent them?"

Kayla said, "I only…facilitate when a person needs to escape their horrible life of terror at the hands of the person who is supposed to care for them. I provide the means for them to start over, but I never know where they end up or how they get there. Only that they are finally safe."

She was going to anger Andis, talking like that. But Conner couldn't help admiring her courage. She knew who she was and that she'd done the right thing. Now she wasn't going to back down from the first threat—even if Andis was likely the worst man she would ever meet.

"I see."

Andis didn't sound impressed. If Conner didn't direct this conversation the right way, it would go horribly wrong. "Andis—"

"I don't think so, Conner." The man took two steps out of reach and shifted his gun. "Turn on the laptop and use whatever program you have to communicate with them to *find my family*." He pointed the weapon at Conner. "Or he dies."

Part of him, honestly, eased. He expected it. Kayla in danger wasn't right. Conner having a gun pointed at him was duty. It was the way things were supposed to be. He should be the one at risk. He *should* be the one in the line of fire. Anything else just didn't sit right with him.

Kayla touched her mouth with her fingers and gasped. He knew she cared, but if he was hurt or killed, he didn't want her to waste time grieving. Not for someone like him.

"Now."

Kayla sprang into action. She set the laptop on the desk and opened the lid. "The computer is *fried*." She pressed the button. After three tries, she looked up. Innocent, but Conner saw something in her eyes. She knew something. "It isn't working!"

Beside the laptop, Conner saw the cord that could be used to connect the damaged laptop to the desktop. That had to have been how it connected with the internet.

Kayla was stalling. Relying on him to figure out how they would get out of this.

"This isn't something I will tolerate," Andis said. He stared at Conner. "This woman has taken my family from me, and if she doesn't know where they are…well, I don't need her. Do I?"

"Just let her go. We'll figure out how to use the laptop to find your family," Conner said, desperate for a way to get Andis to release Kayla. "I'll find someone who can get the information off it."

Andis's eyes narrowed. "This woman has stolen from me. And if she cannot return what she has taken, then I will take from her. A life for a life."

He wanted Andis to take his instead. Conner was trained to take the bullet rather than let someone else get killed. Especially someone he cared about as much as he did Kayla. His body itched to move. To dive in front of her.

"Manny will make sure she does it," Andis said. "You can come with me." He glanced outside and yelled, "Manuel!"

"I'm not leaving Kayla."

Andis and Manny passed each other. Andis didn't comment on what Conner had said. He simply nodded to Manny and then waited by the door.

Kayla hugged her middle, too scared to try to hide her fear. Conner was here with her, but she was likely minutes from death. Andis Bamir wanted her dead for helping his wife and daughter get away from him. She'd met them in the grocery store. The sheriff hadn't been involved at all. First it had just been coffee and talking. Getting to know each other enough that Sofija knew she could trust Kayla not to betray her confidence. Her daughter had been so sweet and so pretty, even with the bruise on her temple. Like a skittish puppy at the pound, Sofija had reached out to Kayla expecting to get slapped back for it. Instead Kayla had shown her the same love and grace she'd been shown by the Lord.

Then she'd helped the woman escape her life of fear. And Kayla would do it a thousand times over, even if it meant her own death. Even if it meant Conner turned her over to Andis every single time—whether it was what he'd done, or not.

She should run, but Kayla didn't know if she could move. She should scream, but she didn't know if a sound would come from her mouth. Her body was frozen, and probably her vocal chords, too.

Andis continued, "My business has been destroyed from within, and there are many culprits. Some trying to buy their way back in using that laptop or by installing surveillance in your office to buy my favor." He looked pointedly at Kayla. "Now is the time to tie up loose ends." Then his deadly attention moved to Conner. "Betrayal cannot be tolerated."

A phone rang, but Conner didn't move. Andis left, and Manny strode across the room, his gun hanging loose in his hand. Casual, as if he wasn't about to take her life and make it so no one ever knew the real story of what happened to her.

"Let's go."

Kayla shook her head. *Don't let them get you in the car.* Her mind flashed with images from murder documentaries she'd seen. Gruesome pictures. Andis's wife's and daughter's visible injuries and the emotional turmoil that Kayla had been unable to see. There was no way she was going to become an evidence photo. A case number on some detective's desk, bringing all the media exposure that went with who she was. No, thank you.

Lord, help me.

She didn't think Conner had betrayed her, but she couldn't look at him either. His gaze would likely mirror all the terror in her heart, and she didn't want to see it.

Manny kept moving toward her. Conner didn't; he just stood where he was. Not doing anything, but looking like he was waiting for something.

A car engine revved. *Andis.* Dissatisfied with

the nonanswer she'd given him, he'd taken off and left her here to die. What kind of a man did that so casually? She didn't see those traits in Conner, which meant there was still hope left that she could point out to him. Why did he wonder if he was a bad guy? He had restraint. Andis had none, which worried her since it didn't seem he would stop searching for Sofija and her daughter.

God, keep Sofija and Lena safe. Wherever they are.

She'd been honest when she told Andis she really didn't know where they were. That was the point of what she did—and how she did it. Anonymity, safety. Two of the most precious commodities to someone who was hiding and fearful for their life.

Luxuries Kayla didn't have, considering everyone knew who she was.

Perhaps this was the only logical end. Not that she would have chosen differently. Secret Service agents were willing to die for what they believed in, and she'd always thought them so noble. Not just Conner—every single one of them. Whether they worked on the presidential detail or not.

Now she would do the same thing.

Kayla lifted her chin while the car outside

sped away. Manny came close enough to reach out and touch her.

Conner launched toward them. His arm whipped out and he grabbed for Manny's gun. He pulled Manny into a spin and punched him in the face. Manny flinched for a second, then brought the gun up.

The tussle began.

Both men fought for the gun, Conner's hand around Manny's wrist as he tried to keep it from aiming at either of them. Shoulder to shoulder, they wrestled for control of the firearm.

"You can't stop me." Manny bit out the words.

Conner's teeth were clenched, and neither man backed off from their struggle. "Andis isn't here anymore."

"Exactly," Manny grunted. "Guess I'll have to say it was an accident. He already doesn't trust you, so I'll tell him the golden boy got in the way. Bye-bye, Conner Thorne." The two men continued to grapple. "Once you're buried, it'll be back to business as usual. Before *you* came along."

Didn't Conner have a gun? He needed to shoot this man! But Conner kept trying for Manny's weapon, while the man continued jeering. "Guess I'll have to prove I was right that you were the plant. Fooled everyone, but not me. You're Secret Service and you always will be. Fired or not."

"Man, you have some serious issues." Conner used his body weight to shove against Manny's shoulder. "Let me guess… Your older brother was a football star, and no one even noticed you."

Manny roared, renewing his fight against Conner. They were evenly matched, similar in height and weight…and strength. And both of them had only one goal: getting to the gun.

If Kayla had to guess, she might wonder if Conner didn't have as many issues as he accused Manny of having. But she wasn't going to hang around and see their battle play out to its only possible end—one of them getting injured.

Kayla inched toward the door, each tiny movement only a breath of space apart. Her heart didn't want to leave Conner, but she needed to go and get help. Her phone was in the car. She could call the sheriff.

Manny looked up. His eyes locked on her.

Conner used the distraction to his advantage. He grasped the gun and yelled, "Go, Kayla!"

She didn't think about it. She just ran.

Kayla rushed into the daylight, down the steps and toward the car before she realized she no longer had to take Secret Service orders. But she knew she needed to get to her phone and call the sheriff. She'd left it in the car so it wouldn't go off when she was trying to be stealthy. Now that precaution might mean Conner's death.

Kayla yanked open the door and jumped into the car. He'd stashed the keys in the cup holder, so she started the engine and grabbed her phone from the floor of the backseat. *Please, God. Get help here quickly. We need You. Conner needs Your help. Don't let him get hurt.*

Kayla fumbled to enter her passcode.

No signal.

She tried to dial anyway, to tell Locke to get here *now*. What else was she going to do? The phone beeped angry tones at her. Kayla threw it on the passenger seat and put the car in Drive.

Where was she going to go?

A gunshot rang out.

Kayla clapped her hands over her ears and screamed. Her foot slipped off the brake and the car jerked forward.

TWELVE

Fire burned the outside of Conner's thigh as though a knife had swiped across him, front to back. His head swam, but he fought the rush of nausea down. If he hit the floor, Manny would put another bullet in him—this time in his head.

Conner let go of the gun and punched Manny once, as fast as he could, in the stomach. He grabbed Manny's ears, pulled his head down and planted his knee in the man's face.

Manny's outcry was cut off like a needle had been lifted from a vinyl record.

Crash. The car—his car—swung in an arc in front of the office and took out the stairs in the process. Shards of wood exploded as Kayla screeched to a halt in front of the door. The passenger window lowered and her gaze connected with his. "Conner!"

He glanced back at Manny, facedown on the floor and out cold.

Conner took a step on his leg, testing if it

would hold his weight. He got as far as the door, grabbed the frame and slumped onto the floor. He scooted forward and dropped into the car through the open window, like a race-car driver.

Kayla gasped. "You're hurt."

The injury wasn't even on her side. It was on his leg by the window, but blood had spread quickly to soak his jeans. He fingered the tear in the denim. It wasn't bad, only a graze. "Don't worry about it—just drive."

She did. But not without glancing at him before she pulled onto the road. "Where do you want me to go? Is Manny dead?"

"No, but when he wakes up, he's going to come looking for us so he can finish what Andis told him to do."

"So where do we go?"

Conner wanted to touch her, but there was blood on both of his hands. Instead he dialed Locke's number. It went straight to voice mail. Either the man was in a dead spot with no signal, or his phone had died—which Locke would never allow to happen.

Conner dialed Greg. When his handler answered, he said, "Andis and Manny got away."

"Why didn't you stop them?"

"Where's Locke? He was supposed to meet us there."

"Traffic report says the crash was a bad one.

An old man was airlifted from the scene." Greg gave him the address to a safe house. "It's actually a vacation rental. Totally clean, and the owner isn't on-site."

"Okay." Conner sighed.

"You okay?"

"Fine." He hung up.

"You aren't going to tell him you got shot?"

Conner didn't answer her. He relayed the address Greg gave him. Thirty minutes later she pulled into the drive, and he told her the code for the detached garage set away from the house. The property was ringed by trees, giving them privacy.

Kayla looked concerned, which wasn't good. Conner wasn't a project or someone she needed to save. He just needed a bandage, some painkillers and about twelve hours of sleep. After that, he'd be up and running again. Kayla didn't need to look at him like she was worried he was going to bleed to death.

He heard the roll of the garage door as it lifted. The car moved, and then Kayla had his door open. "I can help you."

Conner grabbed the door frame and pulled himself out of the car. She slipped under his shoulder and wrapped her arm around his back. How she was going to hold him up when he outweighed her by at least sixty pounds was anyone's guess. They walked slowly together out from under the detached garage's door.

Kayla let go of him for a second and he heard the door roll down and hit the ground. Then she was back, holding him up. They crossed to the front door. Hopefully, there'd be a first-aid kit. Conner's head was pounding. Swimming. He could barely think. Apparently his "just a scratch" was worse than he'd thought.

"There's a keypad lock, not a normal one with a key. We need another code to get in the house."

"Sixteen hundred."

Kayla's lips curled up into a smile. "As in Pennsylvania Avenue?"

He nodded. "I wouldn't have thought Greg had time to set that up. Maybe Locke had him get the code changed. So much for flying under the radar."

She entered the code and let them inside. "What is your deal with Locke?"

Apart from the fact that he'd been the one to tell Conner that Kayla was out of his reach. "He's a good team leader, but he's good because he gives orders that can't be questioned no matter what. And he's always right. It's kind of frustrating." More like infuriating, and not something Conner appreciated. He was a freethinker, someone who adapted on the fly. Locke was way too cut-and-dried for him.

Inside, the house was pristine but smelled like it hadn't been aired out in a few weeks. It made his head swim. He'd rather open all the windows and let a summer breeze in. They walked past a painting—a farm table and apple pie. "I love the smell of apple pie."

Kayla started to lower him onto the couch but hauled him straight again. "Hang on a second." She came back seconds later with a towel that she put under his leg to protect the couch. "Did he punch you in the head? Maybe you have a concussion." She fingered his forehead, his hair.

"You're concussion girl." She didn't smile. It was just blood loss, making him woozy. "Check the bathroom cabinets."

"Afterward you can tell me what that 'apple pie' thing was."

She really wanted to know? Kayla's footsteps retreated. Conner let his eyes drift shut, but the pain wouldn't allow him to sink into oblivion. When he heard her come back and felt the snip of the scissors as she cut away his pants, Conner roused.

"If I hadn't seen you sleeping with my own eyes, I'd wonder if you've rested at all since you came in my office."

"It wasn't much."

"You're fading fast." Kayla's gentle voice drifted around him. "Apple pie?"

"The painting." He waved in the direction of the entrance hall. "I was born on a farm. My mom made apple pie, and the sun used to warm up the living room." The whole place was decorated like a farmhouse. Maybe he should get one, make a permanent home for himself. "My sister would dance in the sunlight, and the puppy would sing."

"What happened?"

"Foreclosure. My dad's gambling debts. They broke his legs. My mom went to work. My sister got into drugs and I haven't seen her since she left. She was sixteen. I joined the air force, then after that, the Secret Service."

Kayla blew out a breath.

"Sometimes I think it might have been a dream," he said. "Sometimes I wonder if you're a dream."

Kayla stared at him. Conner's face should have been relaxed with sleep, but it wasn't. He was always alert, as he was even now. As though his body refused to let him be anything except what he was trained to be.

Conner was no dream; he was very real to her. Maybe even the most real thing she'd ever had in her life. Despite all the trappings of having lived in the White House, of her parents' money and the schools she had gone to, Kayla had never wanted those things. Sure, it was nice not to worry about whether she would eat tomorrow—as so many of the women she helped told her they did. But she had never craved notoriety. She much preferred her quiet little small-town life.

My mom made apple pie.

How was it that she'd known him for so long and hadn't known he'd been born on a farm? Or that he'd been in the *air force*. That seemed like a key piece of information that had completely slipped by her.

She didn't know anything about his family except what he'd told her just now. Yet he knew practically everything about her. Of course, most of it was public knowledge. But everything in her now ached to know all there was to know about this man. Who he was and why he would choose a line of work that put him between a bullet and the person he was protecting.

Why he'd give his life for her.

The front door burst open so fast it slammed into the wall. Locke strode in, a look of thunder on his face. Kayla shot up.

"Where is—"

"Shh." She met him halfway, the team of three men and one woman right behind him.

Kayla pushed at the huge black man's shoulders until he stopped. "You all have to be quiet because Conner is out."

Locke didn't move, and his expression didn't change.

"He got shot." She pulled on Locke's arm. "Kitchen. Now."

Locke glanced back to the woman, a new agent—probably a rookie—Kayla hadn't met. "Perimeter."

The agent sighed.

He glanced at another of the agents. "Go with her." That left one more in this four-person team. Locke barked, "First aid."

Kayla shared a smile with the female she'd like to get to know. The woman's reaction to Locke's orders seemed a little too personal. Locke was even frowning at her, which was great. He needed someone to ruffle his feathers. Kayla liked the woman already, even if Locke had banished her to the "perimeter."

Kayla dragged Locke all the way to the kitchen and opened her mouth.

The female agent spoke before she could. "Your man in here is awake. I think he might shoot me." The front door shut.

Kayla rushed back to the living room. Conner's eyes were open. He said, "What?"

"Locke is here." Conner tugged on her hand

and she sat back down, this time way closer to him. Had he heard her? "How is your leg?"

"The screaming, throbbing one or the other one?"

Kayla's lips twitched. "Okay, enough said. Are you okay...other than that?"

He hadn't let go of her hand yet, and now he gave it a squeeze. "I'm okay, Kayla. It's nothing that hasn't happened before."

Kayla didn't even want to think about that. Undercover work couldn't be easy, and she had certainly complicated things for him.

Locke cleared his throat.

Kayla stood. "I'm going to forage for first-aid supplies. Don't be mean to him while I'm gone."

"Me?" Locke's brown face split into a wide smile.

The smile was for Kayla alone. The minute Locke turned to Conner, his amusement dissipated. "We were stuck behind that accident, and this nowhere hick town has crappy cell service. If I didn't know better, I'd say someone was conspiring against us."

"Andis did show up at exactly the right moment."

"Probably tracking your phone. Or Kayla's."

Conner said, "We didn't figure it for a setup. There was no one there, and she was supposed to just grab the laptop so we could leave. It's still there, dead battery and a destroyed keyboard, but there was a cord out where I think they'd connected it to a desktop."

"We need it?"

"If we keep it under wraps, that keeps the wife and daughter safe. Even if it's been accessed, we can still minimize the collateral damage."

Locke nodded. Conner wanted to shift in his seat, but not only would it seem like he was nervous—which he'd never admit to his former boss—it would also hurt.

"You should have told me you were undercover."

"It's supposed to be a secret," Conner said. "That's why it's called *covert ops*."

"And it was necessary for you to take Kayla along with you?"

"I'm not helpless." She stood in the doorway, holding a red metal box with a white cross on it. The male agent was behind her. "Conner and I have been working together."

Locke turned to Conner. "She stays here from now on. Twenty-four/seven protection."

Conner gave a short nod. Did the man think he was going to argue with that? "Done."

"No. Way." Kayla handed the first-aid kit to the agent and set her hands on her hips. "I'm going wherever you go, Conner. We're supposed to be a team."

Except he'd never actually said that. "Kayla—"

"I'll give you guys a minute." Locke left the room, trailed by the male agent.

She raised her gaze, eyes rimmed with tears. "Don't give me the speech."

Conner jerked his head. "The speech? What speech?"

"It's my job, Kayla." She did an impersonation that might've been meant to sound like his low, gravelly voice. "I'm supposed to keep you safe, that's all. Nothing else."

Conner's chest shook. She was hilarious.

"It's not funny. I never understood why anyone would want to jump in front of a bullet to protect me. My life is no more valuable than anyone else's. I'm not worth that." She shook her head.

"Your father's position put you at risk. That was the job, Kayla."

"That's all?"

She deserved the truth. "Until about three seconds after I saw you the first time. Then it was all about the distance I had to put between us. I had no other choice or I'd have been fired. It wasn't a secret how I felt about you."

"I didn't know. All I knew was that you were

so overprotective. All you guys are. I could barely breathe. I didn't want you to protect me."

Then what had she wanted? "I told Locke not to put me on your detail. Sometimes it couldn't be avoided, but he tried his best to keep us separated. We figured it was better than me breaking protocol because of how I felt."

Conner lifted her hand in his and tugged her closer. There wasn't far to go before they were face-to-face, their noses almost touching. "That was then," he said. "This is now. Understand?"

She had to know that everything was different now. His whole world had changed now that she was in danger, and more than just physically. He was seriously at risk of falling all the way for her. He couldn't help it. He'd never been able to help it when it came to Kayla Harris, as much as he'd tried to fight it. And he *had* tried.

Kayla nodded. Conner's lips curved into a smile. "Why do you look like you just got handed down a sentence?"

"Just accepting the inevitable. That you and Locke are going to gang up on me so you can go out and play heroes while I'm hidden away." She folded her arms.

"That wasn't what I was talking about." When her lips moved into an O, he said, "You don't want this?"

He would back off if she asked him to. She

was everything he wanted and exactly what he shouldn't have at the same time. Would he ever move past this spark? He was determined to protect her, and she would hate his getting hurt for her. But he wasn't going to put her in danger. Not again. For once, he voluntarily agreed with Locke.

"Kayla?"

Her gaze flicked back and forth over his face. Then she leaned forward and planted her lips on Conner's.

Every thought in his head disappeared. He pushed past the surprise and gathered Kayla into his arms for the sweetest kiss of his life. And it was about time, too. So long as he didn't let his head barge into the conversation with the passel of doubts sitting back there.

"Time's up." It was Locke. "The sheriff is here."

Kayla pulled back, her cheeks pink.

The sheriff frowned when he saw her. Conner sent the man a look of his own. "How did he know where we were?"

"I called him," Locke said. "Greg told me everything." Which meant Locke had wanted the man close. Probably where he could keep an eye on him.

Conner didn't need the sheriff's opinion clouding Kayla's potential happiness. He was pretty happy himself, and he wasn't going to let anyone ruin that for her. Conner pulled her into his side. "Jan Barton?"

Sheriff Johnson shook his head. "The motel room was empty. She didn't check out, but all of her stuff is gone."

THIRTEEN

"What does Jan Barton have to do with Andis Bamir?" Locke scratched his chin.

That was a good question. Kayla looked at him and shook her head. "She came to the sheriff for help, and he referred Jan to me."

"And the boyfriend who took your laptop?"

Conner's attention shifted to Locke, as well. "I think he might be the one making superbills for Andis. It's a huge operation with multiple people involved, especially on the scale they were flushing bills onto the market. Jan must be linked to that somehow, even just through her boyfriend. It seems like they're all invested in finding Andis's wife and daughter. As far as I can piece together, they actually disappeared not long before production of the bills halted for whatever reason."

Locke folded his arms. "If they aren't making counterfeit bills anymore, why send you to investigate?"

"It was right after I showed up. Stalled out the whole investigation and made this thing take months instead of weeks. I'm still not done. But it seems like the answer is somewhere between Andis, Jan Barton, and the missing wife and daughter."

"They were being hurt, and now they're gone. It's just bizarre that everyone wants to find them. Andis maybe, but Jan and the boyfriend?" Kayla shook her head. None of this made any sense. "I just can't see how Sofija and Lena could be tied to the counterfeit money. Sofija never said anything to me about that, and we talked about her husband's business. She wanted me to be prepared if he ever came looking for her. Oh, she also said she had an 'insurance policy' in place. That's what she called it. Some kind of comeuppance against Andis for what he did to them."

"They have something of his." Conner shifted beside her and winced. "Something everyone is trying to get their hands on."

"For Andis?"

He nodded at her. "That's the only explanation I can think of. Andis's wife made off with something he needs back. Not a good insurance policy, but she has halted all production of counterfeit bills. If she wanted to mess with him in the process of leaving, she's done it. But now everyone is after her and her daughter. She must think she's totally safe and that Andis won't be able to get to her. Or if he does, she'll either buy her way out with him or turn him in."

Then he looked at Locke. "And they all think Kayla knows where the woman and her daughter are." He sighed. "Let's go get the laptop, see if anyone is still there. Maybe Jan Barton or the boyfriend—"

"That would be Tim Harmer," Sheriff Johnson threw in.

"Maybe they'll show up there."

"I'll stay with Kayla," the sheriff said.

Seriously? Conner was just going to leave her here? Not that she needed his protection, but if she was going to get some, it might as well be him. It wasn't like he was fine, after all. He'd been shot.

Kayla prolonged their time together by helping him clean and put a bandage on his leg. She didn't want to leave the shelter of his arms, but she'd been standing by herself for years. Why cave in now, when she'd been doing so well? Especially for a man who would risk his life.

Kayla spoke quietly so only Conner could hear. "Are you seriously just going to leave me here?"

He didn't react to her tone, just whispered

back, "I need to talk to Locke about some things. Clear the air."

"Is he mad he didn't know about the operation?"

Conner shrugged one shoulder. "Doesn't matter if he is. It's not his purview, not while he's director over the presidential detail."

She pushed away from Conner and stood. "Fine."

He could go wherever he wanted. She hadn't needed a Secret Service detail for years, though it had been an option for her. Kayla hadn't wanted that kind of notoriety when she'd gone to law school. She hadn't wanted to be that student again, the one followed around by suited men and women all day and night. So she'd forged her own path on the understanding she could call Locke whenever she got an inkling something was awry.

Well, things were definitely awry. That was for sure.

She should call her father or have Locke fill him in first and then call. If her father heard about what was happening before she or Locke could explain about Andis, he wouldn't react well. Her father's health wasn't good. If he got a shock from the news because they didn't relay it right, he might even have another heart attack.

Locke was better at that. She should ask him to set a time to contact her dad.

Okay, so she was using Locke as a go-between. But it wasn't like she and her father had the greatest relationship. When she was able to, Kayla needed to visit his house and see him. She didn't want her life to be a cliché of missed opportunities to say what should have been said. What needed to be said. She was grown-up enough to admit she hadn't been the best daughter, and now was as good a time as any to rectify that.

Okay, Lord. I got that message loud and clear. Kayla smiled to herself. She didn't want any more epiphanies like that. She wasn't sure her heart could take it.

"Guess that's it, then." His voice was gruff. "Be back soon."

Kayla glanced at him. Conner ran a hand through his hair. Why did it seem as though he didn't want to leave? Kayla gave him a small smile and waved. He really did look like he needed a nap. *Funny.* She was starting to sound like him.

Locke motioned to the door. "Let's go."

"Or you go, and I take Kayla somewhere else."

Locke's eyes widened. "You want to run?"

She turned to him. Conner wanted to leave

with her and disappear? He would never bring down Andis or Manny if they did that. And yet Kayla fully believed that his personal directive to see to her protection above all else would override the assignment that brought him here. The infuriating man. Of course he would think whisking her away was the right answer.

He turned then and saw her. Kayla shook her head. She mouthed the word *go*. But Conner still read everything she was thinking. She intended to stay here, to fight this with everything she had. Conner didn't like that idea one bit; that was plain enough on his face. He was keeping his idea to run as a possibility. A fact she didn't like.

Conner's lips twitched and he shook his head. They were never going to agree, were they? She could see it coming a mile away. If they ever actually gave a relationship a shot, they'd be mired in couples counseling forever. Never agreeing on anything, and each convinced his or her thinking was the right thing for both of them.

Despite the sweetness of the kiss they'd shared, Kayla simply couldn't see a way this was going to work.

Conner shook his head again and waved her over. "I'll be back soon."

She wanted to go to him again and get another

hug. To see if, maybe, he would kiss her again. But she stood where she was. She couldn't help but think of all the reasons they were doomed. Not just because Manny was after them and she had to hide here. Not just because Andis Bamir wanted her dead and her shelter house was at risk. But because she and Conner could barely seem to agree on anything.

Instead she just nodded. "See you soon."

"What's your take on Jan Barton?"

Conner watched the scenery rush past. Locke was driving—of course—which left Conner and one of the male team members to enjoy the view.

Locke couldn't let anything go. Least of all the fact that one of the last things Conner had done before he'd been "fired" and went under-cover was punch the man in the face. It had been part of the cover story, but Conner couldn't say he hadn't seriously enjoyed doing that. Locke was so smug, so know-it-all sometimes it was infuriating.

"I only met her once," Conner said. "She played the part well. Bruised-up face, cradled her arm like it was broken or something. If it was a ruse designed to find out where Kayla sent Andis's wife and daughter, it was well thought out. She had it down, and she was perfect. Kayla took right to her, even in the middle of everything that was going on. But I knew something was off and I never mentioned it. Too much else was going on."

He told Locke about the break-in at Kayla's office. The director probably knew, but Conner gave him the version that let Locke piece together Kayla's mind-set. Even the best Secret Service agent couldn't protect someone whose mental state was volatile or even distressed. Erratic behavior risked people's lives. They had to partner up with the people they protected, or it didn't work.

Locke took the turn Conner indicated. "She always did feel too much."

He wasn't wrong. Still— "That isn't a bad thing. It's just who she is."

Locke didn't answer.

If Conner had to admit it, he was the same way. *So much heart*, his mom had always said. Like that was a good thing, watching his sister walk away even as she self-destructed. Undercover work had been good for him. He'd had to learn how to be hard. How to shove the care he had for others, for human life, to the side and put work first. Duty had become second nature—that was the life of a Secret Service agent.

What Kayla saw as his innate need to protect her above everything else was only his need to keep her safe. If anything happened to her, or anyone else he was supposed to be protecting, it would destroy him. Especially if it was Kayla. In guarding his heart, he'd created this default mode in which there was only Kayla and the need to keep her safe.

She thought that was a bad thing. For Conner, it was the *only* thing.

Because he couldn't even bear thinking about the alternative. He'd seen burned-out agents. Or agents who let the frustrations of the job get to them. He'd even seen a good agent destroyed when the charge he was protecting was killed. If it was Kayla who got hit, Conner wouldn't retreat from life. He would cease to exist.

Locke pulled into the construction site. The sun was setting and cast long shadows across the dirt and buildings. A dark figure shifted between swatches of black. Conner cracked the door before Locke even stopped. He hopped out and moved away from the now-crawling car. Locke yelled, "Hey!" But Conner ran toward the figure, which ducked behind the construction office.

No one was there. Conner spun around, scanned the area. The window! The office window was open. "Inside!" Hopefully, Locke heard and wasn't planning on scolding him for jumping out of the car before the director could formulate the plan. It could be a neighborhood kid, a thief, but then again, it probably wasn't. He was past the point of believing in coincidence.

"On it!" Conner heard Locke yell back to him over the sound of the car engine.

Conner grabbed the edge of the window and peered over the frame. Inside the office, Jan Barton gathered papers from the file cabinet, got the laptop and turned to the window. Her face was hard, her eyes dark behind the bruises still as fresh as the last time he'd seen her. What kind of woman had someone beat her just to convince the sheriff and Kayla that she was helpless and needed saving?

The answer: a woman who saw the payday at the end of the tunnel.

There were few things in the world that motivated people more than the idea of a bunch of money coming their way. Conner had seen it again and again—the latest example being Andis.

"Hands up. Drop the stuff." Locke stood by the door. "Secret Service."

Conner hauled himself up to the window frame. How she'd climbed inside so easily he didn't know. His leg hurt, bad. And he needed to lose some weight. He sat on the frame and drew his weapon to cover Locke.

Jan Barton glanced between them. One side of her mouth curled up and she smirked. "Boys, boys, boys. This isn't going to end well for you. I need this laptop, so back up and let me leave."

Locke gave a short shake of his head. "Put the laptop down and put your hands up. Now." He might not be so practiced at making arrests, but the man wasn't doing too badly. Though his sheer size made him look completely intimidating. Conner was a little scared of him right then.

"The ruse is up, Jan." Conner wasn't going to let Locke have all the fun. This was his case. "Sofija and Lena aren't going to be found, and whatever part you're playing in this operation ends now."

Jan's gaze flicked from Conner—actually from behind him through the window—to the door. She stood completely still for a second before gunshots began. *Pop. Pop.* "Down!" Locke yelled over the loud cracking sound. *Pop. Pop.*

Conner fell in through the window and hit the floor. Fire shot up his leg and he grunted. Some kind of rifle, probably a hunter's gun. He moved to lift himself off the floor but more shots went off. Bullet holes spread across the back wall. The shots were coming from outside the door beyond Locke.

The other agent was outside. Was he okay?

Jan Barton was down, too. Between shots she

stood up. "Okay," she said into a phone. The laptop in her other hand, she rushed toward the window behind Conner. He grabbed her foot as she passed.

"Jan, stop!" However careful they were, she was going to get hit. "You aren't leaving!"

A gunshot smacked the wall inches above his body. He jerked and her foot left his grip. Jan brought her heeled boot down on the bandage on his leg.

Conner cried out. Bright lights flashed across his world, blinding him. He heard an "Oof" and someone fired.

"Stay down," Locke called. He jumped over Conner and went out the window. Conner got to his feet, pushing down the swell of nausea. The rifle fire had stopped, but that didn't meant the person didn't still have him in his—or her— sights.

Conner hugged the wall, got outside and tried to think where he'd be situated if he was the sniper in this situation. The trees were too far, at least for the kind of accuracy the shooter was getting in the office. Conner's leg was bleeding again, but he could take care of that later. The apartment building being constructed had enough cover.

He drew his weapon and ran...right into a man leaving the back of the building.

"Hands up." Conner aimed his weapon.

The man dropped the rifle and lifted his hands, a reflex. A dark look crept over his face. It was Tim Harmer, Jan Barton's boyfriend, who had stolen the laptop from Kayla. Tim ducked his head and rushed toward Conner as if to tackle him.

Conner shifted the gun in his hands. When Tim came within reach, he slammed it down on Tim's temple. The man dropped to the ground.

"You're under arrest."

FOURTEEN

Kayla couldn't hold it in. She tried, but the tears came anyway. Emotional reactions weren't logical. Like the one she was having now after being left alone—except for the two Secret Service agents outside and Sheriff Johnson, none of whom were Conner. Sitting here, supposedly resting and instead doing nothing but wondering if he was even going to make it back. Or what else would happen before Andis was caught and they made sure his wife and daughter were safe forever.

Since Conner had shown up in her office, Kayla's whole world had flipped upside down. If it ended with her attending his funeral and seeing him in that suit...

That "hero" dive, she could still see it in her mind. He was probably running through a hail of gunfire right now. Putting it all on the line for her. The noise that came from her throat sounded like a growl, even as tears flowed unchecked down her face.

"Excuse me."

Kayla spun around on the couch.

Sheriff Johnson's eyes widened and he lifted both hands so his palms faced her. "Whoa." He cleared his throat, like he didn't know what to say. Or where to start. "Is…everything okay, Kayla?" He sat on the armchair across from her. The agents were around, or one was. The female was outside.

She sighed. "Fine." The word was short. She couldn't give him anything other than exactly what she was feeling. Mad. Not that the sheriff deserved that, but couldn't he see she was in the middle of a drama? "Okay, so everything isn't fine, but it could be." Unless Conner had his way, in which case nothing would be right again.

She should walk away now. Just get in the car—Conner's car—and leave him here. She'd be free, and she'd have plenty of time to find someone normal. Someone who wouldn't insist on taking a bullet for her—because there wouldn't be any bullets. She'd have a nice, peaceful life instead.

He started to get up. "You have a lot on your mind. I'll leave you to it."

Okay, so now she was just being rude. Kayla

had never liked the couple of times when she'd been like that. "I'm sorry. You're right. I do have a lot on my mind."

"You know, if it's not too forward and you don't mind me saying, you once told me that perfect love casts out fear."

Kayla blinked. "That was…"

He nodded. "One of the hardest cases I've ever had to deal with." Not only had there been an abused spouse, but a child had been involved. A child who had been the victim, one neither of them had been able to save.

The sheriff said, "You reminded me that God's love can heal anything, and I got to share that with the mother. Before she…"

Kayla nodded. "You did?"

"Sometimes we need to search outside of ourselves to find something bigger. Stronger than us. Love that can heal even the hurt that goes so deep it rips at the fabric of who we are."

Kayla squeezed her eyes shut. She'd seen it over and over, and she'd thought she knew what it would feel like, but the reality was that she didn't. "Thank you." She smiled at him. "I'm also worried about the shelter."

"Have you called over there? If Andis has you in his sights, it isn't a stretch that everyone there could be in danger."

Kayla nodded. "I think so, too, but Jeremiah

Fallston lives there. He might be eighty, but he used to be a PI, and before that, he was a cop. He only moved here from Norfolk fifteen years ago."

More than once he'd seen someone he didn't like loitering near the shelter or sitting in a car on the street watching the place, and he'd called the sheriff. He saved the women who lived there from who knows how much extra heartache they didn't need.

Sheriff Johnson said, "So you're sure the house is protected from being found? There's no way they can find the shelter, because Jan was never taken there? You dropped her off at the motel, right?"

She nodded. "It's not connected to me in any way. Jeremiah Fallston is a middleman, and there's a house manager, too. I gave him an unregistered phone that we use to contact each other. He sends the manager over."

She gave the sheriff a commiserating smile, knowing how hard burner phones made his job. She hadn't been all the way comfortable with it, but Locke had insisted on certain things— like the phone and using a dedicated email address. "Not even the money or my calls are connected."

It occurred to her that he'd never asked about it before. Kayla could be cautious with what she said, but Sheriff Johnson had been instrumental in helping so many women in town escape from bad situations when they needed to. He would never do anything to jeopardize the good work they had done.

"Very good." The sheriff nodded. "Still, might be a good time to call that middleman and double-check everything."

"I will."

He handed her his phone, which Kayla was grateful for. She had no idea where she'd put hers, and the sheriff only wanted to help. Kayla could feel the remnants of tears on her face and swiped them away. There was something about crying that made being angry so much more satisfying. She sent the sheriff what was probably a crazy-faced, blotchy "I'm still mad at something" smile. "I'm going to call now."

The sheriff nodded and stepped away to give her some privacy, leaving her alone on the couch. Before she made the call, Kayla closed her eyes. *God, I need Your love. Fill me with it so that it overflows, and help me show that love to others.* Most of all, she wanted to show it to Conner. To be the one who drew him to the Lord. *Help me do that, Father.*

Kayla sat in the quiet and prayed for Conner, for everyone at the house, and asked God to keep Andis's wife and daughter safe. Sofija and Lena didn't deserve to feel any more hurt and pain. They should be free of him if they wanted to be.

Peace settled on her like a warm blanket on a snowy morning. She smiled to herself and said a quick prayer of thanks before she dialed the number. Three digits in, the door opened. Conner strode in with a distinct limp, followed by Locke.

"You're back." She stood, aware of the rush of excitement at seeing him. Would that ever calm, even if she saw him every day for the rest of her life?

Conner nodded, then glanced at the sheriff, who appeared from the kitchen holding a mug. "Got a suspect for you to question at your office. We sent a black-and-white of yours over there with Tim Harmer."

The sheriff put the mug down without taking a sip. "Righto. I'll get over there."

"I'll drive," Locke said. "We need to find out what's going on. We need to know why Jan Barton is spearheading this and why it seems like she has a vested interest in finding that laptop."

"Got it."

"And I want your files on all of them. Everything you have."

The sheriff nodded, and Kayla passed him his phone. Before they left, she put a hand on

Locke's arm to stall him. When he looked at her, she said, "Can you check on the house for me?"

He nodded. "I sent the team over there before we came inside. They'll make sure it's all fine."

"Thank you."

Locke and the sheriff left the room.

Conner turned to her, a smirk on his face. Kayla had to laugh, but the humor didn't last long. "He hasn't changed one bit, has he?" She sighed. "I was just about to call the house, check on everyone."

"Jan got away with the laptop. I guess Locke is going to find out why." Conner limped over. "Come on. Let's cook dinner, and we can think about something else. Once Locke gets back, we can plan our next move." He shot her a look almost identical to the one from just a second ago. "You know Locke won't let us decide anything without him."

Kayla smiled. "True." She did need a break. "What's on the menu?"

"How about something easy, like spaghetti?"

Kayla shrugged. She was more into therapeutic baking. Cookies. Cakes. Lemon bars. Or maybe it was more like therapeutic eating. She probably shouldn't admit to Conner that was how she dealt with stress. He'd probably find a bakery and commandeer some sweet treats with the weight of his badge just so she could eat them.

"What just happened to your face?"

Kayla laughed, remembering the first time he'd said that to her. His quirks were cute now, instead of frustrating. "Nothing. Just thinking about dessert."

He nudged her shoulder. "I'm sure we can work something out. We eat, and we take a nap. Sound good?"

Kayla nodded. That sounded great.

Kayla lasted through the first ten minutes of the movie she'd picked. Now she was curled up on the other end of the couch. He'd felt good—as good as he could feel in the heat of danger when he was the one who had to save her—just hanging out with her. He'd needed the rest as much as she had, but Conner could hardly believe what had happened. Cooking together, sharing a meal and watching a move.

It was so simple. Easy things that made up a good life, and doing them with Kayla made him feel like a hero. The concept had dawned on him as she drifted off, a low chuckle of humor in her throat at something one of the characters said. He'd been shocked breathless for a second as he comprehended the enormity of what this meant.

He could come home from a day of fighting the tide of crime sweeping this country, of doing his duty, and find as much satisfaction at home. He didn't have to be a hero at work only; he could be one with Kayla—and not because he stood between her and death. It didn't have to be a compromise or a trade-off. He could have it all.

With Kayla.

Conner was fighting sleep when Locke returned. He stood and met the agent at the door. "Shh."

Locke gave him a weird look.

"What?"

"Nothing," his former boss said. "Tim Harmer won't tell us anything. But we did find something out when we dug deeper into their backgrounds." He paused. "Get this. Jan Barton was in the army. She was on a team that specialized in bomb disposal."

"That isn't good."

"The women's shelter is guarded, and the team is checking for devices. I told them to keep their eyes open."

Conner nodded. "Good. We should check here at the safe house, too."

"I'm going outside to do that now."

"I'm hoping between the laptop and Andis, Jan hasn't had time to make an improvised explosive device. An IED is not something I want to deal with."

Locke said, "It's a new world. The gunman on the grassy knoll isn't our biggest threat anymore. It can come from anywhere, including a radio-detonated bomb inches from the target." He shook his head. "We have to completely change our thinking or we risk POTUS or anyone we're protecting because we aren't prepared for a new kind of attack."

"It isn't a world I want to raise a family in, but what choice is there?" Conner was too tired to temper what he was saying.

Locke glanced at Kayla. "She can handle it. Otherwise you wouldn't even consider a family with her."

"It isn't like I'm considering anyone else. Or that I ever have." Conner shrugged. "It was only Kayla. Always."

Locke nodded. "Guess I'll have to take your word for that. At least until it happens to me."

Conner wasn't sure it ever would, not when the man was so stubborn he'd probably refuse to see what was right in front of him.

Locke glanced at him, then barked a laugh. "Guess I know how you feel about that."

"So what now?"

Locke shrugged. "Rest is good. Keep watch."

Conner opened his mouth to speak his agreement, but Locke's phone rang.

"Agent Locke." He turned his body slightly

away, then went completely still. Like he'd been frozen. "Sheriff—" His words cut off. "Hello? Can you hear me?" He lowered the phone.

"What is it?" Conner asked.

Kayla stirred on the couch and got up.

Locke glanced between them, then put the phone on speaker. "Sheriff?"

Bang.

Kayla's hand slipped into Conner's. Locke looked up, his gaze dark. "Let's go."

Five minutes later Locke pulled the SUV into the parking lot of the sheriff's office. Conner sat in the back with Kayla. Locke got out, and Kayla moved to follow, but Conner held on to her hand. "Stay here with me for a minute."

"Okay." She looked up at him, expectant. The car's interior lights went dark. "What's up?"

"I just don't want you in there until Locke says it's safe."

She grinned. "So we're out in the open and not inside with cover?"

She was right. "Good point. But the SUV is bulletproof, so we lock the doors and no one's getting in."

"Of course it's bulletproof." She reached down for her purse and started rooting around in there. "Where did I put my phone? I lose the thing every time I drop it in here. But you're a guy. You just don't get that stuff vanishes in a woman's purse no matter how often you clean it out."

"Why are you in avoiding mode? I haven't seen that one in a while. Last time, I was trying to convince you not to go to that concert, and you only wanted to talk about why hair spray was better than mousse. I'm pretty sure your speech lasted half an hour." Conner thought for a second. "Because we're in danger?"

"Because I'm in danger *with you*."

"I said I'd protect you."

Kayla folded her arms and glanced out the window. "I don't want to talk about that."

"I gather that. I'm just curious as to your re-action. You know I'm a Secret Service agent, that I would give my life to save someone. It's just who I am. It's how I'm built." He glanced around, but no one was close to them. "You don't have to worry, Kayla."

"I *don't* want to talk about this."

"Because you don't like the idea of being saved?" It dawned on him. "Because you don't want me to get hurt." Conner nodded, mostly to himself. "Because you're falling in love with me."

Kayla's head whipped around. Her emotions, already so close to the surface, erupted. "I am not! You are so self-absorbed. Like I should be grateful you'd die and leave me here!"

Conner could have smiled, the sense of satisfaction was so great. "Because you'd miss me if I was gone." She'd pine for years for the lost love of her life, leaving her unable to function in normal society. Good—that meant she felt the same way he did. "You would. You'd totally miss me if I was gone."

She made a face. The angry tears were coming again. "You'd like to think that. Like I said, self-absorbed. You just want everyone to think you're *all that*."

Conner flicked his head. "Not everyone. Just one person."

"If you think for one second dying is a good idea, I will hate you for the rest of my life."

His mouth crooked up on one side. "Guess I'm sticking around, then. For pretty much ever. Sound good to you?"

Kayla apparently wasn't done being mad. She shrugged one shoulder. "Suit yourself."

Conner laughed. Kayla Harris was probably the one woman in the world who could throw him attitude two seconds after he'd had the sweetest moment of his life. She was falling for him, just like he was falling for her.

"Here comes Locke."

The agent opened the back door and leaned in, his face grim. "The sheriff is dead. And so is Tim Harmer."

FIFTEEN

Kayla tried to breathe deep. She could smell it—that was what hit her the most. It wasn't right. It just couldn't be. Death should be as peaceful as it was final, but this mess was an abomination. She took two steps back toward the front door of the sheriff's office, but it wasn't enough. She needed *air*.

Kayla whirled around and raced to the front door. Conner caught her before she stepped outside. "It's not safe outside unless we check first. Go in that room." He gave her a gentle push onto the chair in the interrogation room. "Head between your legs."

Kayla groaned but did it. Sheriff Johnson and that other man were dead. She tried to feel something for the one who had slammed her against the truck and stolen her laptop, but she couldn't. There was nothing she could do except feel for the sheriff. The grief of a friend's death—a good man who had looked over this town, who had encouraged her earlier that night. Someone who had helped her with the women and children who lived at the shelter, referring her cases and helping her keep the whole thing confidential. Now he was lying dead on the floor, and Conner wouldn't let her see it whether she wanted to or not.

She listened while Conner talked to Locke about things she didn't even want to hear. She lifted her head, not knowing if she wanted the answer but needing to ask anyway. "What did they do to him?"

"Two shots to the chest. If Jan Barton was in the army it could have been her. There's a lot of blood, but that doesn't mean it was sloppy like a gut reaction. Whoever fired those shots meant them to be dead."

"Why would someone do that? Just to silence Tim? They didn't have to kill Sheriff Johnson, as well. They could have left him alone."

Conner touched both his hands to the outsides of her arms. The look on his face was soft, and she realized she was breathing too heavy.

Kayla inhaled and held the breath for a second. When she had regained some control, he said, "Jan is still at large. We have to be more careful than ever now."

Kayla scrunched up her face. There was nowhere safe, nowhere that they could go that

Andis wouldn't eventually find them. What was the point in being careful? They would only end up the next victims.

Conner ran a hand through his hair. "Don't give up on me now. We can prepare for what might come since we know Jan—and Manny and Andis—are out there still. We'll stay vigilant while we figure out a plan with Locke to get Andis."

"They'll come after the house. They'll try to find Sofija and Lena. I can't let him hurt anyone else. Sheriff Johnson is dead."

"I know."

She ignored the softness of his words and stood. *How much more will You ask me to handle, Lord? I don't think I can take much more. I'm breaking, and I don't know how to get through it.*

Kayla paced the length of the interrogation room.

"We have to stay here until Locke is done. After that, we can head back to the house."

Protect them, Lord. Just like You protected me. You sent Conner to save me, and now You brought Locke to help both of us.

The sheriff hadn't had that, despite whatever faith he'd had. Faith wasn't a guarantee of safety. Everyone still had to live in this world—a crazy beautiful place full of messed-up people all trying to live their lives. And selfish people who only wanted to please themselves.

Kayla lifted her chin. "Who will make sure the town is safe now?"

Maybe she should move the women's shelter. Could she uproot all those people, send them from their place of safety to another location they weren't familiar with? She had to consider the trauma some of them had been through. Could Kayla move them now and make the manager explain that they were no longer safe? Did she have another choice?

She sighed. "I'm sorry."

He frowned at her. "For what?"

"You're all doing so much to make sure everyone else stays safe, including me. All I seem to do is scream and run with you wherever you take us."

"You've helped plenty, Kayla. You got us out of the construction site when I was shot and drove us to the house."

"Your handler got that safe house for us to stay in."

"Don't discount the part you've played in this."

"You mean causing all of it?" She saw his face. "No, don't give me that look. It's true. I'm the reason you haven't been able to complete your mission. Now I might have messed it all up."

"So?"

"What do you mean, 'so'? It's important."

"More important than you being safe? Or the women and kids who live in the shelter?" He paused. "Because I'll tell you, it isn't. Nothing is more important to me or this job than your protection. That's how it is, Kayla. Not a result at the expense of anything else. I don't operate like that."

She knew that. Mentally she knew, but did it make things better? He had to get Andis, and now Manny and Jan Barton, too. Kayla liked to think she could take care of herself, but the last time she was in a terrifying situation without Conner there—at least before this all started—she'd only managed to grapple with the guy long enough for him to show up. And that was years ago. Since he'd appeared at her office, she'd managed to get some hits in, but the reality was that she hadn't even been able to keep her laptop safe.

If she was cut off from Conner somehow, would she even survive the next time? Tim Harmer was dead, but there were way worse people after them. This man was happy to die for her, but what would he do if it was Kayla who died to protect *him*? Her tendency to create a catastrophe was leaping off the charts, and she needed to rein it in.

Conner watched her pace the room. It was clear that Johnson's death had rocked her. Her emotions had run the gamut from one extreme to the other, and he didn't envy her having to feel all that. Conner had kept himself separate from other people for so long he didn't really remember what it was like to be friends with someone.

Then along came Kayla.

The only reason things between them were going as well as they were was that it was her. She didn't want him to die, but she didn't get that, as it had been for the sheriff, death was a very real possibility in his line of work.

She stopped pacing and pinned him with a stare. "I want to go to the shelter."

Conner stepped closer to her, but Kayla backed up. "I know what you're going to say. I know it's the best thing to stay away. They have enough protection. But I promised them they'd be safe, and they're not. Right now it's only a threat, but it could become so much worse before we catch Manny and Jan. And bring down Andis."

"None of them know about the house. Jan might have killed the sheriff and Tim, or it could have been Manny. We won't know for sure until the evidence is assessed." He motioned toward the main area of the sheriff's office, where Locke was. "This could be Andis just as easily as Jan. Or one of his other men."

He didn't want to tell her that it was possible the sheriff had been tortured. If he'd told his killer about the shelter, then it was in imminent danger. Had he known where it was?

Locke had called his team. They were prepared, and they would defend the shelter. Kayla didn't need to worry about them.

Conner had more questions than answers. Andis's wife and daughter were long gone, but the house Kayla had set up was still here. What would be the point in Manny terrorizing them? Would Andis destroy those people's peace just for the sake of one-upping Kayla? And they still didn't know why Jan was so invested in all this. Whether she was the one who silenced her boyfriend, or if it had been Manny.

"Hey!" Locke's voice boomed through the sheriff's office. "Hands where I can see them! Get them up!"

Conner pulled her back and went to the door. He palmed his gun. The man who'd entered stood in the door, both hands raised. Conner tilted his head but didn't move his gaze from the man. "It's Manny."

He felt Kayla's hands grip his shirt from behind. "What does he want?"

Conner called out, "What do you want, Manny?" Locke hadn't ever seen the man, not yet.

"I just came to talk. That's it, just talk." Manny lifted his shirt and turned in a circle so they could see he had no weapon.

Locke still had his gun trained on Manny, so Conner lowered his. He didn't holster it, just kept it by his side. Quietly, he said, "Stay in this room, Kayla. Don't come out where he can see you."

She pressed into his back for a second and then stepped away.

Conner crossed half the room, careful to stay out of both the sheriff's blood and Locke's line of sight, and moved to Manny. The coroner was due soon, and local crime scene technicians. The place was going to start buzzing with deputies and reporters as soon as word got out that the sheriff was dead.

The deputy on duty was due back soon, and no one had found the dispatcher. The others who worked for the sheriff were on their way in. Conner hoped they wouldn't walk into a gunfight.

"Did you do this?" Conner motioned behind him to where the sheriff still lay.

Manny dragged his gaze from the sheriff's prone body. "They got Harmer, too?"

Conner nodded. The man's body was still in his cell. They hadn't even unlocked the door, just blasted him through the bars. "You know who it was?"

"Andis ordered it, but it was Jan, I'd guess." His expression didn't change. "The old man is scrambling, trying to find Sofija and Lena." There was a spark when he said Sofija's name. "Jan bought her way back in—I have no idea how. Unless I kill you, I have no standing."

"Is that why you're here? To kill me?"

"I'm done working for him, playing the part. Sofija and Lena are in trouble and I want to help them."

"Why now? What's changed?"

"I didn't know about the laptop. I didn't think Kayla would actually have a way to contact them. Now that Andis got what he needed from Jan, he has the laptop and he's cleaning up loose ends. Didn't want Tim Harmer talking. I'm guessing the sheriff was just collateral."

"And the pharmacist?" Conner didn't trust anything the man said but was willing to listen if it fed them more information. "Trying to kill me at the construction-site office?" Conner motioned to his leg.

"Andis's orders." Manny winced. "I'd say

thanks for putting up a decent fight, but…" He shrugged.

"You shot me in the chest."

"You were wearing a vest, weren't you?"

"You're gonna have to explain this," Conner said. "Because I just don't believe you've had a change of heart."

Manny stared. After a minute of quiet assessment, he said, "Sofija. She was supposed to call and tell me that she was okay, that it was safe. I was going to join her." He took a breath. "I'm putting all of us in danger, telling you this. Andis is on a rampage about her. He thinks Jan is going to lead him to them, and I'm scared he might be right."

"You're scared?"

"Yeah, Conner. I am. Sofija and Lena don't deserve this. They just wanted a better life. I didn't want to go unless it was free and clear." His eyes hardened. "I won't live a life looking over my shoulder. I knew about what Kayla did, so I told them when she'd be at the grocery store. It didn't take much to secure them a ticket to a new life. With some insurance."

"What was it?" Kayla had mentioned Sofija having said something about an "insurance policy." "What does she have on Andis that makes him want to find her so badly?"

Manny shrugged. "I don't know. But he's mad

like you wouldn't believe and determined to get her back. Everything is falling apart."

"Wow," Locke interjected. "That was a great story, but I didn't believe a word of it."

"Sofija and Lena are in danger."

"We know," Conner said. "What we didn't know was that you were having an affair with your boss's wife." He wanted to roll his eyes. No honor among thugs. "And now, after playing your part expertly, making us think you were trying to kill us, you're inclined to change your tune and act like the concerned third party."

"You're under arrest." Locke stepped forward.

Conner did the same. "There are multiple things we can charge you with, but I'll settle for having you off the streets so you can't do any more damage under Andis's reputation. You're done, Manny."

"They're in danger," the man sputtered. "You have to help them!"

"We are. And part of the reason they're in danger is because of you coming after Kayla."

"I was helping distract Andis! Jan and Tim were the ones hurting people!"

"You shot at me and Kayla," Conner said. His voice sounded hard even to his own ears. "Now you won't hurt anyone else."

"But they missed their check-in."

Conner caught the cuffs Locke tossed him. "They should have called by now!"

Kayla huddled in the interrogation room. That man scared her so much. He wasn't the one who shoved her against the truck—that was Tim—but he had terrorized them over and over again. Was she really supposed to believe now that he had cared about Sofija and Lena all along? That he'd been waiting to know they were safe before—what?—joining them?

She watched Conner lead the man away from her, purposely shielding her from anything Manny might potentially do. He was determined to be the hero, and she loved him for it. Kayla knew that now. She wasn't falling for him as he'd said. She was already gone.

But she didn't want him to act the hero if he was going to give his life for the cause. Nothing was worth that.

Not even her.

He needed to live. To have a full and long life, happy with a family—kids. Whether they were hers, too, or not didn't matter, did it? Nothing mattered more than him being loved and finding peace. Conner was a comfort she hadn't realized she'd needed before now. When her mom had died, her father had wanted space, so he'd left her alone. What difference would it have made if she'd had someone to lean on?

Kayla supposed they were a lot alike. Each willing to do whatever it took to see the other have a future. But that would come later. When this was over.

Kayla's phone rang. She didn't recognize the number. "Hello?"

"Kayla Harris." Jan Barton's voice was like flint. "All these women and children, so scared." Someone whimpered in the background. "They don't have to be, if you do every single thing I tell you to. If you don't, I start shooting them. One by one until you fall into line. Understand, *Ms.* Harris?"

SIXTEEN

Kayla couldn't think. Conner had told her to stay put, but she needed air. Kayla shoved her way through the sheriff's office until she collided with Conner. She clutched the phone to her ear and took in great heaping breaths. Her head spun, and the world threatened to flip on its axis. How could Jan do this? She was supposed to be an innocent in need of help, and now...

"Did you kill the sheriff, Jan? Was that you?"

Conner's head whipped around to Locke. He let go of her with one hand and snapped his fingers. Locke returned from locking up Manny and got out his phone. But how would making calls help? Jan was holding all those women and children hostage. Thirteen people whose lives depended on her, who might die if Kayla made the wrong choice. Because she'd thought Jan Barton was innocent.

"What do you want?"

Jan chuckled through the phone. How could Kayla have thought this woman was the victim? She should have known. She should have seen something in Jan that was off. Something.

"Just tell me, Jan."

"Andis Bamir's wife and daughter," Jan said.

"Where are they?"

"I don't know. That's the point of how this whole thing works."

"Then these people all die. Because *you don't know*." Her voice turned shrill. "You find them. You get back the fake bills and watermark stencils they took. I don't care what you have to do, *Ms. Harris*. You get them back, and you do it fast."

Fake bills? Watermark stencils?

Andis had been making counterfeit money, and Jan knew about it. She was involved in the operation and now Kayla was supposed to find a woman who had disappeared on purpose? Andis's wife and daughter had been given what they needed to escape and leave absolutely no trail—though apparently there had been a plan to contact Manny.

If he'd been telling the truth.

Her computer could be used to find them only if they used the email account. Andis would only be able to pull old emails off her account. Unless Sofija used a computer or a phone for some reason, no one should have been able to find them.

Emails, internet use, phone calls. Those were traceable. Kayla had warned them against logging on to social media accounts, contacting friends or even making new accounts. It was best to stay below the radar.

Which meant there was no way to find them. Not unless Andis's wife and daughter drew attention to themselves in some way.

Instead of telling Jan that, she said, "So you can kill them, or so you can make more fake money? Because it's really not my fault you got nothing off the laptop."

"I get to spend the money. And yeah," Jan said, "I do a little killing sometimes. Nothing big, but I get my point across."

"Like Tim and the sheriff?"

Jan laughed. "That was just for fun."

"So I bring Andis's wife and daughter to you, and you murder them? You take back this money and the stencils, and you continue to break the law. Is that it?"

Jan Barton dissolved into cackles of laughter. "Cute. 'Break the law' like it's some big deal. That's real cute."

Kayla wished she could see the woman's face. She wanted to punch it.

"I get paid. That's how this works. I earned

that money, and they'll learn no one takes from Andis." Jan paused. "We get back to work making superbills and everyone is happy."

"Except an innocent woman and her daughter will be dead." Even if she could find them, which she couldn't.

"There are worse things than being dead."

Kayla pressed her lips together. Jan wanted her to be complicit in the death of a woman and child who only wanted a better life—and had stolen from Andis in the process? "I doubt the woman you plan on killing, or her daughter, will be too happy."

"That's the price they pay for leaving Andis." Jan huffed out a laugh. "I wouldn't do it. Not worth it. But then, he needs me."

Kayla squeezed her eyes shut. She'd taken Jan's word on faith and it had turned around and bitten her. Always believing the best, always trusting that the innocent were the ones who needed protecting.

Hadn't Conner taught her that people weren't so simple as to be "good" or "bad"? Not all one thing all the time. People were far more complicated than the labels they were stuck with or the categories society placed them in. Each one was an individual. And she had put them in harm's way.

"All these sniveling women. Kids screaming." Jan groaned. "It's starting to bother me."

And she was going to react by killing them. "Let them go, leave them all alone, and I'll find Andis's wife and daughter for you."

"How about I stay here until you do that, instead?"

Not that it was a question. Jan was giving her no options. "Killing those people won't make me find them faster."

"Sure it will. That's why they're my hostages."

Kayla gripped the phone. Someone came to stand beside her. She backed up and looked. Conner. His face was soft as he moved close and put his head next to hers, his arms loose around her. Not to comfort her, though it had that effect, but to hear what Jan was saying.

"Don't hurt them," Kayla said, strengthened by Conner's support. "I'll try to find Andis's family, and you can leave the women and children alone. They don't deserve to be pulled into this."

"Because they're so innocent?"

"They're trying to start over, the same way Sofija and Lena are trying to start over. Give them all the chance to build the lives they want, Jan. If you take that from them, who are you but a bully?"

"Not the first time I've been called that. Good

thing I don't mind, or I might have popped off one of these kids." She was quiet for a second. "Though, they're wailing so loud it's getting annoying."

"Jan! Don't hurt them."

"Find Andis's wife and daughter and I won't start shooting."

"It'll take time." Time enough for Locke to see where his team at the house were, and rescue the hostages. "You'll have to wait."

"Ticktock. Bang."

Jan hung up.

Kayla looked up at him. "She's going to kill them. How do I find out where Sofija and Lena went?"

Conner took hold of her shoulders. "You don't. They don't need to be found for us to finish this. They're better off safe."

"She's going to kill the hostages!" Hadn't he heard that part? She couldn't be responsible for the people she'd tried to save being hurt. Kayla didn't think she would be able to keep doing this if she had put them in danger. *Lord, why is Jan doing this? She deceived us all. Don't let her lies hurt those women and children. Keep them safe.*

Kayla's mind cleared enough that she could ask, "So what are we going to do, if we're not going to help them?"

"Why does Jan want Sofija and Lena?"

Kayla explained about the money and the stencils. Conner's eyes widened. "They have the watermark stencils?" When she nodded, he said, "That means they have the evidence that will put Andis away for counterfeiting. We can get the production of those superbills stopped once and for all if we get those stencils. No one will be able to use them. But we have to deal with Jan Barton first."

"How?"

Conner gestured toward Locke. The man's eyes were shadowed almost completely black when he looked up. "Locke?"

He swallowed. Had she ever seen him at a loss for words? "The agents at the shelter aren't answering."

Kayla said, "Jan has them?"

"Or she killed them." Locke stood like his body was frozen.

Conner shifted so that he stood shoulder to shoulder with Kayla. She grabbed his hand in hers and held on tight. Conner said, "Let's get suited up and go get them."

It took time for a deputy to take over the sheriff's office crime scene. That had been a fun conversation Conner hadn't wanted to have. *Surprise, I'm a Secret Service agent. Surprise, the sheriff is dead.* He didn't envy the deputy having to take over that job. There would be a lot of cleanup on this, but first there were people to save.

Conner glanced at Kayla beside him in the backseat. "I think you'd better pray."

Kayla wrinkled her nose. "If you think it's going to help, then you should pray, too."

He smirked, though there was little humor there. "Maybe I will."

"Good."

Conner's lips twitched. Faith was important to her, and if she was going to spur him on to being a man who went to God with his needs, he was glad for it. Being a Christian would only make him a better person, so what was there to lose?

Conner said a silent prayer, mostly just to keep his word to Kayla. If God could pull through for them on this, Conner knew He would on everything for the rest of their lives. He could find out more about what that meant after he took care of this mess.

Kayla tapped Locke on the shoulder. "Take the next left."

Locke gripped the wheel so tight Conner figured when he let go, there would be grooves from his fingers. Conner prayed for the agents at the house, that they would be safe. He prayed for the women and children there, that Jan Barton wouldn't jump the gun and start shooting. They needed time to get there and coordinate a rescue operation. He had to figure out how to keep Kayla safe outside while they went in.

What to do with Manny.

How to bring down Andis for good.

How to neutralize Jan Barton without anyone getting hurt in the cross fire.

Prayer flowed, though he kept the words in his mind. It had taken him a long time to get to this point. To surrender and finally admit he needed help. This was over his head. Even with part of a team to work with, he still couldn't handle all the things that might go wrong.

Locke turned the corner without indicating. He shut his lights off and crawled down the dirt road toward the ranch house. Kayla had done well finding a house that was secluded and yet close enough to town it didn't take emergency services twenty minutes to get there.

Lights were on in the living room. Two vans and a truck had been parked along the circle of the drive, but no one was outside.

Locke parked the car out of sight and turned off the engine. "We're cutting it close for us to breach before Jan Barton starts getting impatient." He shifted in his seat to face Kayla. "If she calls back, try to stall her. Ask questions.

What does she know? Where does she think they might have gone? How much money did Sofija take? That kind of thing. Okay?"

Kayla nodded, her eyes on the house and her fingers nervously smoothing out the rumples in her jeans. Conner grabbed her hand and shot her a smile. His body hurt, and no doubt hers did, too. Neither of them needed to be here right now. They should probably be seeing a doctor, not preparing to conduct a raid to save a bunch of hostages.

She returned his smile and then looked back at Locke. "Is it just us? Shouldn't we have help, a team or something?"

"My team is here somewhere. I doubt Jan Barton managed to best them, but we have to find out what happened. Why they aren't answering phones."

"We?" Conner asked him. "Kayla will be in the car."

Locke shook his head. "We need her help. She stays with you—you keep her safe. She can get everyone out after we've cleared the place." Locke handed Kayla a gun. Smaller than both his and Conner's, it fit perfectly in her hand. "You remember what I taught you?"

She gripped it with confidence, as though she respected the weapon, even as she lifted one eyebrow. "I still don't like guns."

"Just because you don't like them, doesn't mean they can't kill you."

Locke climbed out of the car.

"Are you sure about that?" Conner motioned to the weapon.

Kayla gave him a half smile. "I'll only use it if I have to."

Conner nodded and they got out. Night had fallen, and wind whipped through his hair. The breeze ruffled his collar against his neck. Was Kayla okay? He glanced back. Was she cold? Conner shook his head. They could worry about that after. When she wasn't in imminent danger.

He didn't agree with Locke's decision to include her. Conner prayed it was only Jan Barton in there. Kayla wouldn't be in danger then, because she wouldn't get in Jan's line of sight. He would make sure of that. Problem solved.

They passed a car, blue with government plates. Conner cracked the passenger door and looked inside. Blood had pooled on the driver's seat.

"Locke."

"I see it." But he didn't stop. Conner and Kayla followed as they made their way along the edge of the drive.

Finally, Locke slowed and lowered to a crouch behind a truck. "Okay, tell me about the house, the outbuildings. Everything."

Kayla explained the layout, then pointed to the barn. "That's mostly storage for farm equipment. They have a garden, and they grow a lot of vegetables and fruits. Berries, stuff like that."

Locke glanced at Conner, who nodded. "Let's check the barn first." The Secret Service detail could be holed up in there if they had a man down. Then again, they could have been found and killed. They could be hostages. There were just too many variables as to why they weren't answering their phones.

Locke led the way again. Conner put Kayla between them, and they raced in the dark to the barn and around the back to a small door.

Locke pushed it open a couple of inches and looked inside. Relief relaxed his body. "Guys."

Inside the barn, two agents sat with a third bleeding from his stomach. The relief on the female agent's face at the sight of Locke was profound. And interesting.

"What happened?" Conner put his arm around Kayla.

The female agent flushed. "It was my fault. I thought she was one of them. They kept coming out with snacks and coffee. She hit me." The agent touched the back of her head and winced. "Then she fired on the guys and ran off with all of our phones, guns. Ammo. We have nothing. I was just about to start out and go get help when you showed up."

Locke said, "She wanted entry to the house."

"It's worse than that."

"What is?" Kayla asked.

The female agent kept her gaze on her team leader, her chin high as she faced Locke. "She wired the house. Trip wires and C-4. If we go in, the whole place will blow."

SEVENTEEN

"I was in the air force. I won't be much help diffusing bombs," Conner admitted.

The female agent shot him a grin. EMTs had snuck in and taken the injured agent to the hospital—no lights, no sirens. At least until they'd been out of earshot of the house.

This tiny county had no bomb squad. The sheriff's department personnel were all tied up with the sheriff's death. Locke had decided they weren't going to involve them when emotions would be high. And the closest team of federal agents was three hours away. The best they had were the people in this room, which thankfully, wasn't too shabby.

Locke motioned to the two remaining agents, one of whom had blood on his shirt and hands. "You saw her set the bombs, right?"

"Some of them."

The female agent nodded. "Trip wires. She connected them so they wrap around the whole house. Even if we get past the circle, who's to say she didn't wire all the doors and windows after she was inside. And I think I saw others, too. Males."

"I can get in."

Conner spun to face Kayla. "Whatever you're thinking, the answer is no."

"It's the best solution." She looked scared, but she kept her chin high. "Jan will open the door if I tell her I know where Sofija and Lena are. If I tell her I can get back the stencils and the superbills they stole. You know it would work."

"I know you could get shot, and I know there's no way I'm going to let that happen."

Locke said, "I agree with Conner."

"So I do it," the female agent said. "I won't pass for Kayla up close, but if we swap clothes… I could wear a hat to hide my hair." The agent touched her temple and the dark hair there. She had to be Hawaiian, or maybe Native American. The agent continued, "I could get to the door, hopefully inside. I could disarm Jan Barton. Or at least try."

Locke frowned but didn't voice his dislike of the idea.

Kayla said, "I'll call Jan and say that I'm coming inside with information about where they are. To trade for the hostages' freedom."

Conner nodded. "It could work."

The female agent said, "Or at least get me inside the door. If I distract Jan long enough, you guys can sneak in, too."

Locke shifted his stance, the frown still on his brow. "It puts everyone at risk if we get in and Jan has a bomb in the area where the hostages are."

"She said she'd start shooting," Kayla said. "She didn't say she'd blow them up. Maybe she only set the bombs outside like traps. To alert her when someone approached the house."

Locke nodded. "It's overkill if it is true. I'm not in the mood to clean up pieces of you guys if this goes wrong."

The female agent took it in stride. "Good, because I'm not in the mood to *be* pieces." She strode to the window, and Conner glanced at Kayla. She gave him a "What on earth?" look. Something was going on with Locke and the woman agent. Only Locke seemed to not be aware of it.

Locke motioned to the door. "Us guys will go walk the perimeter. See if there's a way to get to the house while avoiding setting anything off. You ladies get ready."

Kayla closed the small distance between them and Conner opened his arms. They shared a hug, and he kissed her cheek. "I'll be back."

Kayla nodded her head. "I'll call Jan while you're gone, tell her I found them."

"Less information is more, remember? You only need to convince her it's your information in exchange for the hostages and that you'll only do that in person. She doesn't have a different choice."

Kayla blew out a breath and nodded. Conner leaned down and gave her a quick kiss on her lips, just because he wanted to. Then he let her go and walked out. He liked this plan, the one where Kayla stayed in the barn. Safe. And the rest of them went inside.

Locke and the other male agent worked on the bombs outside. When Jan had disarmed the door to let the agent posing as Kayla in, Conner watched her enter.

Conner and Locke stood back from the front and back doors respectively while the third agent stayed with Kayla. They wasted no time entering the house. The female agent would have only seconds between entry and Jan Barton realizing she wasn't Kayla.

The light over the oven was on, as was the oven. Dinner had been forgotten and left to burn to a crisp. Conner crept past the long wood table and into the hall.

A man turned the corner, and Conner rushed him before he could pull the trigger, slamming him against the wall. The gun erupted. Conner's breath hitched in his chest, and for a split second he wondered if he'd die or if Kayla's God would see fit to spare his life for the thousandth time.

He punched the man's face, wrestled with him and finally settled for slamming his head back against the wall. The man fell to the ground in a heap. One of Andis's men.

Boots pounded the wood floor through the room on his right. Conner waited until the last second and then shoved the door as hard as he could. He heard the collision, then the cry of alarm as the man on the other side fell to the floor.

The searing heat of a recently fired gun touched the back of his skull. Conner whipped his head out of the way and the gun went off in his face with a crack and a flash of light. Blinded, he flung his fist out and connected with the hard wall of the man's chest.

Two hands shoved Conner back. He stumbled but kept his footing. The man lifted his gun, but Conner brought his up at the same time. His service weapon, not the unregistered illegal weapon he'd carried for Andis. He aimed at the man's chest and the guy did the same to Conner with his more powerful weapon. Both shots would be point-blank range. They would shoot each other, but maybe this guy didn't want to die.

"Don't do this," he said in a breathy voice. "Walk away and I won't kill you. You don't have to die for Jan Barton." Conner sneered. "Put the gun down and I won't take you in."

"I knew it. I knew you weren't one of us. I could smell it on you, but Andis didn't want to believe it. Too busy with the rest of the business to listen when I told him."

"Making counterfeit bills."

"Shoulda known a fed would think he don't stink." The man grinned. "Looks like your job ends here."

"Yours does."

Locke grabbed the man and slammed him against the wall. "You're under arrest."

"Jan Barton?"

"She's down." Locke glanced aside and yelled, "Clear!"

"All good in here, too," the female agent yelled back.

Locke grinned. "Job well done."

Kayla hugged and spoke with each of the residents. They were shaken up but unharmed. The kids needed time to process what they'd been through. Kayla needed to find a good psychologist she could bring over to work with them, to help them move on from it. There would be a lot of nightmares that night.

A young woman with blond streaks and darkness in her eyes came over, and Kayla said, "I'm so sorry," for the millionth time.

The girl hugged her middle and didn't make eye contact. "She was pretty crazy. I haven't been scared like that in months."

"But you're safe now."

The girl shrugged one slender shoulder. "Maybe." Then she wandered off to a group of women, most of whom held babies on their hips. More kids clung to moms' legs.

The lady who managed the house made her way over, a conciliatory smile on her face. "It wasn't your fault."

"But it was because of things I've done."

"And because of things you've done, these women have a home. They have a family who loves and supports them. Some of them are *alive* because of what you do." She set her hand on Kayla's shoulder. "Don't discount that. Good comes with bad—it always does. But we ride it out, and we weather the bad because that's what makes the good all the sweeter."

Kayla swiped a tear from her cheek. The house manager gave her a quick hug, and Kayla made her way across the grass to Conner. The guys had dismantled every bomb after they made a deal with Jan Barton that if she told them how, they would tell the judge and request a lighter sentence. She wasn't going to get off, but there was some wiggle room with what judges could do. It was both appreciated and frustrating as all get out from Kayla's lawyer perspective.

Work seemed like weeks ago. She didn't even know what she'd have to do to catch up. Things at her office were a mess; her life was a mess. And then there was Conner. He was a mess, but *they* weren't. And she was glad for that fact.

Thank You, Lord, for keeping everyone safe and for allowing them to arrest Jan and the men who were with her.

Kayla had been as scared as she was grateful for the female agent who'd gone inside in her place. Even Locke had been impressed by the way she'd taken down Jan Barton without allowing the woman to get a shot off.

She might be a rookie, but she was a great agent who clearly cared about people.

Conner wandered over. "Ready to get out of here?"

Kayla reached for the hand he was holding out to her and walked with him. "How is your leg?"

Conner grimaced. "I'm still moving. Tomorrow it's probably going to hurt like nobody's business. Not looking forward to that."

"No." Kayla's headache hadn't really let up. She was fighting the edge of a concussion still and thanked God it wasn't worse when it so easily could have been. The two of them probably looked like they'd escaped a war zone. Showers. Clean clothes. Sleep. All beautiful blessings God might want to give her soon, or she was going to start turning ripe.

An unladylike snort left her before she could stop it.

Conner lifted his eyebrow. "Do I want to know what that was about?"

Kayla shook her head. They approached the SUV and Conner got the keys from his pocket. "Locke will get a ride with the others later. But we should get out of the open."

Kayla nodded. The danger wasn't over. She needed to quit getting distracted by him and forgetting that. Jan had been taken care of, but what if Andis sent others?

He set off down the long drive and pulled onto the highway. A quarter mile down, headlights flooded the interior of the car from the oncoming lane. From the height of the headlights, it had to be a truck or an SUV. Conner put his hand up to shield his eyes from the brightness.

The SUV didn't pass them, though. It cut left

and screeched to a halt in front of them. Conner slammed on the brakes and nearly collided with the black SUV. Did it have government plates? It seemed like a vehicle Locke would drive. Something imposing.

But Locke would have mentioned if he had other men in the area. "What is this?"

Conner heard his own fear reflected in Kayla's voice. He unsnapped the clip that secured his weapon, just in case. "I don't know."

He glanced over his shoulder and put the vehicle in Reverse.

A van pulled up behind them, boxing them in. The men who climbed out weren't Secret Service. They drew weapons and approached the car on both sides. Conner's door was opened. He lifted his hands on the off chance they were cops of some kind.

"Exit the car, sir."

As he climbed out, he said, "Can I help you guys?"

"We ask the questions." The comment came from behind him. Conner glanced over his shoulder to see a man pull Kayla's arms behind her back. He heard the unmistakable sound of cuffs being placed on her.

"Hey. What—"

Her body was slammed against the car and her words cut off.

"Easy." Conner moved, but a hand planted against his chest, and he couldn't go any farther.

"Leave it alone," the man closest to him suggested.

"As if." He motioned to her. "Get the cuffs off her. Now."

"Not happening." The man beside Kayla pulled her by her elbow and set off back around the car to the SUV.

"Who are you guys?" Conner looked around. "FBI? DEA? Who? You're not arresting her, at least not officially. Cuffs aren't necessary. She's not a flight risk, and she's not someone you can manhandle."

"That's up to us," said the man beside him.

"That's President Harris's daughter. Whoever you are, you better get ready for a backlash you can't even dream of." He tried to move, but the man still had him pinned. "Next month, when you're claiming unemployment, don't say I didn't warn you what would happen if you messed with her."

The man beside Conner smirked. "I'm so scared."

"Conner!" Kayla called his name as they bundled her into the backseat. He couldn't help her without getting past the guy in front of him.

Conner got in the man's face. "Tell me what this is about!" He wanted to know where they were taking her, but that was a good starting point. If he didn't get satisfactory answers, he was going to start fighting. They'd probably shoot him, since he figured if they did have badges, they were operating outside those parameters at this point.

When no one said anything, Conner yelled, "Where are you taking her?"

The man drew his phone out, casual-like, and stared at the screen. "Guess you'll find out."

The blow hit him from behind. Pain exploded through Conner's skull and he fell to the ground.

Before he hit the grass, hands grabbed him and hauled him up.

"Let's go."

EIGHTEEN

The low hum of airplane engines rumbled against Kayla's cheek. She shifted and wiry carpet abraded her skin. Kayla planted two hands on the carpet and pushed up as she opened her eyes. The plane wasn't moving. What on earth was going on? Those men had shown up and arrested her. Then they'd thrown an unconscious Conner in the truck after her. That was when they'd stuck the needle in her arm.

"You're awake. How unfortunate."

She shifted and looked over to where Andis stood with another man. He said something, too low for her to hear, and then the man disappeared toward the front of the plane. A small plane, like a personal jet that seated maybe twenty, two plush armchairs on either side of the aisle.

It was still night outside, and they weren't in the air. She'd been out for a while but not long enough morning had broken.

Much like last time she'd seen him, Andis wore slacks, shined shoes and a button-down shirt. It was like he didn't know he lived in a small town and not a big-city high-rise. He was a slick, moneyed thug who had people to do his dirty work for him.

"What is this?" Her voice was hoarse. "Why am I here? Where's Conner?" Kayla coughed. "I don't know where your wife and daughter are."

"Not to worry, because I do." Andis waved behind him. The woman she'd met only a few times and her daughter sat huddled together. Tied up. Tape over their mouths. Sofija had a cut on her forehead that had bled down her face long enough that her hair looked sticky with it.

Kayla's eyes locked with Sofija's tear-filled ones that gave away nothing but an overwhelming fear. She thought they were going to die here, a fact that hit Kayla all at once. Where was Conner? She couldn't look around, since Andis was making his way over. Was she going to die with them? Why were they on a plane? Was Andis taking them somewhere, so he could kill them there?

"Took some time getting what I needed from that laptop. Your friend Drew was immensely helpful."

Kayla sucked in a breath and prayed they hadn't killed Drew. "What do you want?"

Andis narrowed his eyes. "Nothing you need to worry about. In short order, all this will be complete."

"You'd have let Jan kill everyone in that house just because you wanted your wife and daughter back? Those people haven't done anything."

"You think I have anything to do with that crazy woman?" Andis huffed. "What do I care what she does? Everyone's trying to steal what is mine, and they think they can buy my favor with it? No more." He clapped. "My property has been returned, and it's time to move on. Greener pastures and all that."

Kayla blinked. Was she supposed to know what he was talking about? "You didn't send Jan to hurt them?"

"Too bad for her, and for Manny, I have resources and am more than capable of reobtaining my property when it decides to run away with my money. Jan was helpful enough, but she will not receive the remittance she believes she will." He glanced at the woman and girl behind him. "And I am more than capable of rectifying situations. I'll have a clean slate. A slate on which I will manufacture more money. This time with no partners and no clingers-on to cater to."

"Because they all turned on you?" Even if

she was going to die, she still wanted to know what had happened.

"Jan will get hers," Andis said, without emotion. "Despite being in jail, Manny has already been taken care of." He made a scoffing sound.

Manny was dead? Andis had hired fake federal agents, or real ones willing to break the law for money, to capture Conner and Kayla and bring them to him. Probably they'd been the ones to find his wife and daughter, as well. Now they were gone, maybe even the ones who were "taking care of" Manny. Then Jan.

So much death.

Grief welled up in her, but she shoved it back. This man would not see her break. Kayla didn't care if he saw her mad, though, so she let those tears fall. He thought he was going to kill them? She wiped her cheeks and looked around. Where was Conner?

Kayla saw a jean-covered leg and his shoe sticking out between rows of seats. She ignored Andis and crawled over. Conner's face was smashed against the carpet the same way hers had been.

"Conner," she whispered, scared to wake him up if it would mean he was going to feel his injuries. But she needed his help. She needed him.

"So now what?"

Andis glanced toward the front of the plane.

"I leave. You stay." He waved toward his wife and daughter. "They stay, I go on with my life and the four of you meet your destiny in a fiery crash. So sad. But not so tragic when the police investigators find evidence that you were producing counterfeit hundred-dollar bills and using them to fund your 'altruistic' activities. No one would ever suspect you were in fact part of a group undermining this country's already disastrous economy."

"You can't blame this on us!"

"With the right information planted in the right places, I very much can, you see," Andis sneered. "And I walk away clean, no longer suspected of anything. Answering to no one. It's a win-win."

"You're the only one winning!" Locke knew the truth. The Secret Service would never let him get away with this.

Kayla searched through Conner's pockets—the ones she could get to without Andis noticing her roll him over—for his phone. She needed to call Locke and get him here.

They needed help, before the plane took off and Andis disappeared. His plan was to kill the four of them—and probably the pilot, too, if they were crashing. How could the man walk away from this? He clearly had no conscience and wasn't concerned about anything but what would put him ahead. Money. That was all this man cared about. Money he didn't have to share, because he had all the pieces of the puzzle.

Andis walked away. Lena began to cry, and her mom pulled her to her side so they could huddle together. Kayla wanted to scream. She wanted to fight. She was not going to give up.

Thank You, Lord. Help me know how to fight him, how to survive this.

God had put her there for a reason, and maybe that reason was to help them all live. Kayla continued to pray, asking God for wisdom. To know the right time to move and what to do. Andis exited the plane, and the pilot moved to the door.

"What are you doing?" She jumped up. "You know this is a suicide mission! He wants us to die."

The pilot shut the door, not even acknowledging her existence. How could he do that? Surely he didn't expect to die, as well.

Kayla ran back to Conner and tried to gently shake him awake. The tears came in full force now as the plane rumbled down a runway and they lifted off the ground.

Andis's wife began to wail.

Kayla sank to the floor beside Conner. "You have to wake up. I need you. I love you, Conner, and I don't want to die if it means you're not with me." She wasn't making any sense. "Not that I want you to die, but we're on this plane and it's taking off. It's going to crash with us on it. Conner." She tried to shake his shoulder without moving his head at all. She didn't want to hurt him. "Conner, you have to wake up."

I love you.

Conner's head pounded like a rock concert was going on inside his skull. What had happened rushed back in a flash flood of information—those fake agents, Kayla being arrested. He opened his eyes and tried to focus. White ceiling, curved. Kayla.

"You're awake. I couldn't stop him. I tried, but he left and now we're in the air."

Conner looked around more. An airplane?

"Sofija and Lena are here. They're really scared, and we need your help."

"Help me up."

Kayla did, and she handed him a bottled water, too. Her bottom lip looked red from being chewed on. She kept talking, but the words blurred with the clang in his head. Conner kneaded both his temples and tried to focus. Not cops, or agents on the job, as he'd suspected. Sent there to capture both of them—or just Kayla, and he'd been an added bonus.

"Tell me what happened."

She explained everything from when she

woke up to Andis leaving. Then Kayla said, "Please tell me you know how to break through a locked cockpit door."

Conner didn't answer. He got up and went to the door. The plane was climbing, so the walk was uphill, and he set one hand on each chair he passed to steady himself. Conner tried the door. Locked.

Andis was seriously going to crash the plane? That was insane. Framing them when they couldn't defend themselves. Murdering yet more people. It wouldn't have surprised him if Andis had killed Drew after he forced the man to find Sofija and Lena.

He only wished he had some way now to contact Locke and let him know what was happening.

He banged on the door. "Hello! We need some help back here! We need to know what's going on!"

Could be the pilot was unknowing, and Andis had sabotaged the plane. Or the man had some kind of escape in progress, though how he'd do that was anyone's guess.

Conner banged on the door. No answer.

Anger lit in him like a match to gasoline. He slammed both fists on the door. This was not supposed to be how this assignment ended. Kayla wasn't supposed to be hurt and about to die, and neither were Andis's wife and daughter. Ever since he'd found out months ago that Kayla lived in this town, he'd been distracted. Had his distraction made it so that they all ended up dead?

Conner couldn't even contemplate the fact that he might have been so oblivious to what was going on. Andis had been an impressive catch, a solid win for the Secret Service's undercover operations. An arrest that would have put Conner's name in a category with some of the best agents they had.

Instead he'd go down in history as being an epic failure.

Okay, God. I give up. Kayla said You always help her. Well, we need Your help now more than ever. Show me how to get us out of here.

The door flung open, the pilot slammed into him, and with one *whack* Conner was on his back, staring up at the ceiling. He turned to watch the pilot, who had a bulky backpack— wait, was that a parachute?—on his back. No. He wouldn't leave Conner to—

The pilot wrenched the door open and jumped out.

Wind rushed through the cabin like a hurricane had touched down. Alarms blared from the cockpit. Conner stared at the open door for a second more, then hopped up to his feet. He turned to check on the women, not harmed physically but not happy, and the child was screaming. Kayla looked like she wanted to.

Conner blocked it all out and got to work. He fought his way to the pilot's seat, trying to remember everything he'd learned in the air force. This was in no way the same thing, and he did not have a license. He wasn't supposed to land a small passenger plane under even calm circumstances.

Had Andis known Conner had flight experience? It must have been part of his plan to frame them—to make it look like Conner was attempting to fly them away.

Conner grabbed the stick and pulled on it. Nothing happened. He pushed the rudders with one foot, then the other. No response. The controls must have been disabled somehow to ensure they fell to their tragic deaths.

Lord, help us.

He heard nothing but alarms.

Conner searched around for headphones. He put them on and found what he prayed was the right channel. He radioed in, then gave in to fear. "Hello? We need help."

Nothing but static greeted him through the headphones.

He scanned the scenery outside. They were still climbing, though slower now. They'd reach a point and then simply stall out and fall from the sky. Conner had to get control of the plane if he was going to do anything.

He pressed buttons. Flicked switches. Anything that looked like autopilot, he toggled the switch, hoping for some kind of a response.

He slammed his hands down on the dash.

And saw the fuel gauge.

Empty.

"Kayla!"

She rushed forward. "There are no more parachutes."

"I can't land this thing." What were they supposed to do? "Andis's wife and daughter?"

"They ran to the back. They're hunkered down hoping to survive."

She grabbed his hand. "Is this it? Are we going to die?"

He grabbed the handles and pulled. They couldn't go higher for much longer before they dropped into a tailspin.

"Lord, help us."

Conner had prayed before, and the shelter residents had been rescued. If she thought praying would help now—when he could see no way out but their deaths—he was willing to try it again.

God, we seriously need Your help. Don't let Kayla down. Don't let us die without the truth being known.

The plane dipped for a second. Suddenly they weren't going as high as they had been, or as fast. The dials all moved. The engines, which had been roaring with their fight to keep the plane aloft, cut to an eerie silence. "The engines stalled." He pulled her into the seat beside him. "We're going down."

Kayla gripped his hand and yelled over the sound of the alarms, "We're going to fall out of the sky."

NINETEEN

Dawn was breaking in the eastern sky, but Kayla couldn't marvel at it. The plane had stopped climbing and all she could hear was her own breathing. Short gasps coming fast as the scenery tilted and she caught sight of the ground.

"We're going down." She was repeating his own words, but she couldn't even process what was happening. They were *falling out of the sky.*

Kayla could barely pray, she was so flustered. Nausea roiled in her stomach, and her abs screamed from how tight she held them. They were going to die, and Andis was going to get away with it.

Conner pulled on the joystick thing, hauling it toward him. Nothing happened. They would dive into a tailspin and crash into the ground. Four dead, accused of producing counterfeit money. The fallout for her father would be catastrophic. She hated that it would happen to him, the media smearing her name across the headlines, making her look like a criminal. Like Andis. Every legal contract she'd filed with the court would be called in to question. Every case Conner had ever investigated. It was like ripples from a rock thrown into a lake—the effects would touch so many people.

But it would hurt her father most of all.

Tears ran down her face.

The plane jerked. "What?"

She glanced at Conner. His hands gripped the handle and he pulled. "What is it, Conner?"

"It's working."

Kayla looked at the autopilot controls. "The light went off. It's not on autopilot anymore."

"We stalled. I might be able to get us level again, but this won't be pretty."

"Why did it switch off?" She hadn't meant to say it out loud, not when he was fighting for control of the plane. Kayla gripped the sides of her seat and hung on, praying the belt would hold. Praying the mother and daughter in the back would be safe.

"Could be a safety feature or something. Does it matter? It might have saved our lives—how about we call it a God thing?"

That sounded really good to her. "Thank You, Lord. Help us get to the ground in one piece."

The land around them was farmland, wide

stretches of green fields that might cushion their landing so long as they could avoid hitting a mountain, a barn or someone's house.

Conner turned the plane to the right in a wide arc. He couldn't know how scared she was. It would make him more nervous, and this situation was serious enough. They were going really fast. Maybe too fast.

Kayla looked around. "Is there a road or something we can land on? We need a runway."

"First we need to find out how to get the wheels down."

"What's that?" A black dot in the distance lifted up from the ground and headed in their direction.

"Helicopter. He'd better stay out of the way." Conner flicked switches. She didn't know what they were. "But if that's a local news crew, they'll see us go down. They should contact emergency services. That means an ambulance and fire crews will be on the ground when we land."

Why hadn't she taken those pilot lessons her dad had offered her? She would have known what to do instead of sitting around, not helping, again. *Lord, I'm deadweight. I'm not making a difference here. I only put us in more danger. I can't save Conner. I always have to wait for him to save me.*

But it wasn't Conner who'd saved her; it was the Lord. And He was the only one who could save Conner, too. Whether they lived or died, God had paid the ultimate price to save both of them—He'd given His Son.

Thank You for reminding me of that. She'd been so caught up in her problems she'd forgotten the bigger picture. The one that stretched beyond this life to something more. He'd given her Conner. What a blessing, a gift of protection from the God who loved her.

Kayla had only ever been good at arguing her point. In person or on paper. How was that helpful? But she had discounted herself so many times she'd forgotten the point of a partnership. The kind of relationship that she wanted with Conner didn't mean she would sit there in silence. She wanted him to encourage her, and to spur her on to be the best person she could be. And she wanted to be able to do the same for him.

He'd said that she'd been there for him through all this. That she'd played an important part. Protecting her meant everything to him; it was what made up who he was.

Kayla laid her hand on his shoulder and fought down the fear over what was happening. "I'm sure you can land this plane. I know God will help you, and I'm trusting that He'll guide your hands while you get us down onto the ground."

Conner's focus didn't move from his control of the plane still rapidly descending. They were running out of fuel. From all angles this was an impossible problem, but faith had seen her through so many times she just *knew* God had brought her and Conner together for a reason. They were going to get Sofija and Lena onto the ground safely.

Out loud, Kayla prayed more. For their safety and protection. For Conner to know what to do and to do it at the right time. Peace flowed through her. She wasn't useless, and even though she still just sat beside him and didn't physically do anything, she was helping. She knew it, though he didn't smile. He didn't move his focus. Conner swiftly and efficiently controlled the plane.

A whir of machinery started. The wheels were going down. Kayla prayed more. Conner nodded once, to himself or her, she didn't know. They were lower now, headed for a highway. It looked clear of cars.

The sun had risen above the horizon, washing the sky with an orange glow. God's mercies were new every morning, and she was counting on that fact today.

"There." Conner's voice came out hard and

sharp, as though he was holding the plane steady with the sheer force of his will.

She looked in front of them, where a tobacco field was laid out. They were going to destroy the crop the farmer had planted, but if the four of them came out of this alive, she would pay him back double for what he'd lost. Who cared about holding on to money when they might lose their lives?

Conner moved his hand to the center and gripped a big handle. He shoved it forward by inches as the sound of grinding filled the cockpit. The landing gear going down still? Kayla prayed harder than she'd ever prayed.

The helicopter was close now, circling above them. A news helicopter. Probably broadcasting their plane crash live after seeing them nearly fall out of the sky. Had they called for help? Couldn't they see this plane needed assistance, not an audience?

Conner cried out as he forced the plane to the ground, nose first. All his frustration, fear and hope came out as a great roar and he pulled back at the last second.

The plane touched ground and bounced back up again. They shook side to side in their seats.

Kayla turned to the back of the plane and yelled, "Hang on!"

Her head smacked against the seat cushion.

They hit the ground again, whipping in their seats like pinballs. The plane slowed as they tore through the field toward a fence. The wind screamed as Conner pushed the handle for the brake flaps, and finally, they slowed to a stop.

Conner's chest heaved.

He lifted both hands from the controls as though he couldn't believe he'd done it.

"You did it." She could barely believe it either. "You landed the plane." She looked over, her hand still on his shoulder from when she'd prayed for him.

Conner glanced at her, tears of pure relief and joy in his eyes. "Kayla."

She smiled. "You did it."

"I love you, Kayla."

Conner packed all the emotion he felt into those four words. It was past time she knew how he felt. They'd been through the worst few days he could have imagined and they were alive.

Was she going to say it back? Maybe she'd said it before only because she thought he'd been about to die. Or he'd imagined it. He had been coming around, not all the way conscious. Maybe it was just wishful thinking.

"Conner…" Her eyes softened, but she didn't finish whatever she'd been about to say.

He unclipped his belt. "I'm going to check

on Sofija and Lena. Make sure they're okay."
His body protested and his head still pounded.
It hadn't hurt while he'd been guiding the plane
into that rocky landing that nearly tore the air-
craft apart. Now that the adrenaline was no
longer throbbing through him, aches and pains
answered every movement.

Kayla's footsteps pattered behind him.
"They're at the back."

Not in any seat, though. They were huddled
behind the back row, between the reclined
chairs and a wall of cabinets. Why hadn't they
buckled in?

Conner crouched, trying to hide the wince.
He probably needed to be in hospital.

"Are you okay?"

The mom nodded. She spoke rapidly in a lan-
guage he didn't know.

"There's a fire truck outside and an ambulance," Kayla said. "Let's have them check you
out, okay?"

Andis's wife nodded. "Thank you, Kayla."

Kayla held out her hand, and the daughter
took it. Conner helped the woman to her feet
and they walked as a group to the open door.
Thank You, God, that no one got sucked out.
He didn't want to know what that would have
been like, falling to certain death with no parachute. Landing the plane was bad enough, but

he knew God had been guiding him. There was no explanation other than that the Lord had answered Kayla's prayer.

He'd gotten them down to the ground, and Conner would thank the Lord every day for the rest of his life. When he looked at Kayla. When she said "I love you" back to him.

That hadn't been a dream. He'd heard her say it.

He was going to ask her to marry him. Not now, but when the time was right. Conner was going to convince her to spend the rest of her life making him the happiest man ever, because he knew that's what he'd do for her in return. He would make sure of it, because she didn't deserve anything less.

The firefighters were wide-eyed all through the story, and they quickly ushered the mom and daughter to the ambulance. Conner found a spare patch of dirt and sat down with a thud.

"Conner!" Kayla rushed over the few steps between them and crouched. "Are you okay?"

"I need to make a call." He pulled out his phone.

Kayla waved over the paramedics. Conner dialed Locke's number and put the call on speaker.

The director answered immediately. "Conner?"

"We're good."

"I'm almost there. I heard about the crash. I cannot *believe* you got abducted off the highway." Behind Locke's voice was the white noise of tires on a road. "I saw the whole thing live on the news station's website. Did you seriously land that plane? And Kayla's okay?"

"She's okay."

She leaned forward. "Conner needs to go to the hospital. He's *not* okay."

Locke said, "Conner?"

"Bump on the head. I'll live." Along with the shot he'd taken to his leg and the bruises and scratches he'd acquired. Other than all that, he really was okay.

The paramedic touched the back of his head. He flinched away and wound up nose to nose with Kayla. She was alive. She was unharmed. He had done his job. "We need to find Andis."

"Locke will find Andis. You just worry about you."

Locke said, "She's right. Let me figure out where he went."

Kayla leaned closer and let her weight press into his shoulder. "What about Jan Barton and Manny?"

"Safe and sound in custody. We think there was an attempt to gain access, but my agents took care of it."

"So everyone is good? Andis said Manny had been taken care of."

"I think he tried. We're looking into the attempt. Andis probably spoke too soon."

Kayla sighed. "I'm glad everyone is okay."

Conner wanted to hug her. She felt so much, for so many people. But did she care about him? He thought she loved him, but until she told him when he was lucid, he couldn't know for sure.

"Everyone's healthy."

Kayla slumped against him. Conner put his arm around her to hold her up, but more because he wanted her next to him for as long as she'd stay there.

"I'm pulling in now."

The line clicked off.

Kayla turned her gaze up to Conner's and said, "What? I don't know what that look means."

Conner shrugged one shoulder. He couldn't deny that he was disappointed she hadn't said his words back to him in the plane, but he understood why not. This was a crazy situation, and she probably wanted to make sure he hadn't just knocked some things loose getting hit on the head.

Locke parked. He climbed out, still wearing a tactical vest over his suit. The man probably slept in his shirt, tie and slacks. Cuff links, too,

Conner would guess. But it was good to know some things didn't change.

Kayla smiled at the Secret Service agent but didn't move. Conner shifted her so she was closer against him and smiled up at Locke himself. Sure, he was basically stating his intentions to the entire Secret Service this way, but he wanted it to be official. Kayla was his. In a way, she always had been.

"Kayla." Locke crouched, a frown on his clean-cut dark face. It satisfied something in Conner to see the tint of gray on the sides of his black hair. "How are you?"

"I'm okay."

"We're both okay." Conner lifted his chin.

"He is not." Kayla told Locke everything that had happened, including what Andis had said.

"I figured this was a bigger operation than I imagined," Conner said. "Andis bankrolled it, and he parceled the business out until he knew enough to make the superbills himself. Then he eliminated each player and took off."

Locke stared at Conner for a second. "We'll find him. If he spoofed your phone at any point, then we can try to fake the clone into giving us access to it. Like turning a virus back on the person who created it."

Conner nodded.

"Phone?" Locke held out his hand.

Conner gave it to him.

The paramedic who'd been poking the back of his head set his hand on Conner's shoulder. "You need to see a doctor, but it's not too bad."

Tell that to his pounding head.

The paramedic continued, "Probably hurts a whole lot, but you're not in danger of keeling over."

Conner nodded. "Thanks."

"We'll get the woman and child to the hospital. Both of you okay making your own way there?"

Locke answered, "I'll bring them."

Kayla got up, and Conner let Locke haul him to his feet. He slung his arm around Kayla's shoulders just because he could but also a little because he wasn't so sure about his footing. He'd landed a plane. His nerves were basically shot for a while now.

Locke talked on his phone as they walked. Kayla and Conner climbed in the back of his massive SUV, and Locke hung up. "Greg is going to work on finding Andis."

"Great."

Kayla gave a heavy exhale beside him. "I can't believe it's over. We survived what Andis had planned, and now we can go back to our lives."

Conner smiled. His life was finishing up this

case, locating the evidence and persuading Sofija to testify in return for going into witness protection with her daughter and Manny—if that was what she wanted. Conner didn't like it, but the justice department had made worse deals than allowing someone like Manny to go free in exchange for his testimony.

Kayla's was here in this town, where she'd no doubt be hailed as a hero for protecting everyone she helped with that shelter of hers.

"Do you think Andis will come after us? You're not going to put me in witness protection, are you? Because you know it wouldn't work."

Locke didn't shake his head. The man gave nothing away, while Conner wanted to give Kayla every reassurance he had. Locke said, "Let's cross that bridge when we come to it."

Kayla groaned. "I need to call my dad before he hears about this on the news."

"The agents assigned to his protection have been ordered not to show him any newspapers or let him watch TV. But it's not going to work for long, so don't wait. You can tell him everything yourself, okay?"

"Thanks, Locke." She reached across the seat and Conner took her hand. The back of his head was probably bleeding through the bandage and on the headrest, but he didn't care. Conner closed his eyes.

Locke said, "Wha—"

Conner heard the screech of brakes a second before the truck hit the side of Locke's SUV and everything went black.

TWENTY

Kayla's head swam. Her mouth formed words, but she didn't hear anything. The world was muffled, like she was underwater, but she felt the seat of the car under her. Air, like the windows were open. Gas, like they'd sprung some kind of leak, filled her nose until it turned her stomach. Her head pounded.

Conner. Locke. Were they okay? Kayla couldn't turn her head to find out if Conner was awake or alive. The driver's seat in front was twisted, the door pushed in so that it had forced Locke over. Kayla saw him then, leaned across the center console. Blood everywhere.

Conner was probably dead, too. She didn't even want to look. Kayla couldn't bear to see him that way.

The door beside her—crumpled like a tin can the same way Locke's was—screeched open.

Someone grabbed her arm. Pain whipped through Kayla's shoulder. The scream tore from her throat. Two hands grabbed under her arms and she was dragged away from the car. She tried to look around, couldn't see who it was. Someone trying to help?

Kayla was dropped. Her head hit the asphalt and she blacked out, her body feeling nothing but pain. She rolled to the side and retched on the street.

When she turned back and looked to see who it was, Andis peered down at her. A gun swam before her eyes, his other hand loose by his side. She couldn't see the look on his face, but she knew who it was.

"Look who ruined a perfectly good plan," he said. "Guess I'll have to just shoot each of you and then take care of my family. Shame. Pinning it all on the four of you was a good idea. Now more will die, and you'll be the first. Knowing they will be killed because you didn't die when that plane crashed."

The words swam in her head, and she tried to make sense of them through the haze of pain. If he was going to kill her, he should just do it. She was hurting enough that it would be a relief.

"A messy end." He crouched. "But I'll still get away." He grabbed a handful of her hair and hauled her up. "On your knees. Might as well give the medical examiner something to talk about. Three kills—two feds and the former president's daughter all done execution-style. I'll be a legend. The thug who got away."

She felt the metal of the barrel press against the back of her neck. Kayla squeezed her eyes shut. *I guess this is the end, God. Don't let my father falter over this. Don't let his heart give out. Keep him strong and hold him up with Your strength.*

That was the worst of it. Her dad would need her, and she wouldn't be there to help him. Conner would be gone, and so would she. They'd never get to see what might have happened with time. Never get to see what the future would bring for the two of them. A tear rolled down her face as the magnitude of what they would lose descended on her with the reality of what was about to happen.

She wasn't afraid. No, Kayla only mourned for what might have been.

"Say goodbye."

Kayla squeezed her eyes shut so hard it hurt. *Goodbye.*

"Andis!" Conner's yell made her jerk out of her stance. Kayla fell sideways, her hand slammed onto the concrete and she managed to not collapse. *Conner.* She watched him limp over and then looked back over her shoulder. Andis shifted the gun and pointed it at Conner.

"No!" She didn't want him to die first. She

couldn't watch that ever, and definitely not if it was the last thing she saw.

He didn't look at her, not while his whole being was focused on Andis. "Put the gun down, Andis." He lifted both hands, blood-smeared palms out. Where was his gun?

"I don't think so."

"Walk away, Andis. That's the only way you get free of this, not by murdering Kayla. You want to leave, then leave. But if you kill us first, then you'll be hunted every day for the rest of your life. There won't be a single place in this world where you'll be able to hide. No peace. No rest. No safety. The full force of the Secret Service and every private soldier President Harris cares to hire will be half a step behind you. You won't be able to breathe without giving yourself away."

Conner sucked in a breath, his attention trained on the man with the gun. "Walk away, Andis."

"So that you can hunt me every day for the rest of *your* life?"

"I won't. I'll do nothing. I'll say nothing." He looked dead serious, not at all like he was anticipating his death any second now. "Leave right now and I'll forget you ever existed. I'll tell everyone we don't know who hit us. You'll be clean. Free."

Conner's words came fast, the only tell as to exactly how desperate this situation was. Kayla prayed Andis didn't shoot him. God had aided Conner in landing that plane, and He could help them now, too.

She moved to get up, to put some distance between herself and Andis. He saw and twisted around so the gun pointed at her.

Conner yelled, "Kayla, no!"

She froze, her body in a crouch halfway between kneeling and standing, and stared at that gun. She rose slowly before her muscles shook so badly she fell back to the ground, both hands raised.

Andis had his attention on her—maybe Conner could use that to his advantage. She hadn't planned this, but Kayla decided to improvise if it just might save both of their lives. "He's right. Leave and you won't have three more murders on your conscience. You've already done enough damage, haven't you? But you were a step removed so far. This isn't conspiracy, Andis, this is pre-meditated murder."

He might shoot her, but Conner could use that split second of Andis's focus on her to take the man down.

She would give up her life so that Conner could live. For the same reason he would, because it was the right thing to do. But beyond that, because she loved him more than anything. And that love was bigger than her need to spend her life with him. It might cost her everything, but it was how she felt. Filled with enough love that she would gladly give up her life for him.

It might not be why Secret Service agents were prepared to die for their charges, but it worked for her. And she knew, down to her bones, it was why Conner had wanted to protect her from day one. Why she'd been a liability and he'd had to pull away from her. And why they hadn't been able to see eye to eye.

Andis's face changed—his lips curled up into a sneer and he opened his mouth. Conner moved. His arm, his leg, the muzzle flash. A deafening boom. Conner blocked her view of Andis. His body jerked.

Another gun fired.

Conner hit the ground. Then Andis collapsed. Beyond them Locke stood with his weapon pointed and a hard look on his face. His gun shook, and Locke fell back against the car. He slumped onto the ground.

Kayla fell on the asphalt beside Conner. Blood covered his chest. She took off her jacket and balled it up, pressing it as hard as she could on the wound. "Locke!" He looked nearly dead. There was no way he could help her. She looked back at Conner. "Why did you have to get shot again, when you're not even wearing your vest?"

Kayla didn't want to leave his side, but she scrambled across the ground to the director. Locke was still wearing his vest. His injuries were from the car collision. Kayla groaned. "Please be okay."

She found the phone in Locke's pocket and called for help.

When Conner woke up, he couldn't feel much of anything. He wasn't even sure he had a body, everything was so numb. Until he looked down at the bandages that covered his chest, and the white blanket. Hospital. That meant help had come. Hospital meant an ambulance, which meant someone was left alive to call them.

No thanks to Conner.

Was Kayla alive? Locke? Andis? He blinked and tried to look around, but his head swam, so he gave up. His mouth tasted like an old marshmallow. Conner tried to clear his dry throat. Even inhaling was hard.

He tried to remember what had happened. The car had been hit. Locke, blood all over him. Andis, holding his gun on Kayla. That look on her face, all that love and fear and trust and "Help me" and "Do something." He'd seen it all as clear as though she'd said it out loud.

Something had happened since he had walked into her office. He couldn't deny that, not when it meant he'd done something so dumb. Now he didn't know if she was alive or dead, or if Andis had been caught somehow. Because he'd been bleeding out, unconscious, he didn't have any answers.

How could he have done that? Sure, he'd caught the bullet. But he hadn't stopped Andis. He'd saved Kayla only for that moment and then left her alone to face Andis and his gun by herself. Conner should have found a way to disarm Andis. He should have tackled the man, instead of diving between Kayla and the gun. In the split second the gun fired, he'd made a choice to save her instead of neutralizing the threat. Not that it had been a choice, not really. It was Kayla.

It had only ever been Kayla.

Now she might be dead because of what had happened to him, because of the choice he'd made. Andis might be in the wind, long gone with the means to make more superbills. Conner would spend years tracking him down until he went to prison for murder. The end. Because if he had hurt Kayla, Conner would kill the man. And he'd accept the sentence, because it would not be self-defense. He just wasn't built that way.

Conner tried again to clear his throat. He seriously needed some water, but he needed to know if Kayla was okay first. There should be a button to call a nurse, right?

Someone moved beside him. "What is it?" Kayla touched his arm. He smelled the sunshine and flowers of her perfume and then her face was in front of his. Unafraid but full of a whole lot of concern.

She's here. He tried to speak, but no words came out. Kayla brought a cup to his mouth and Conner drank from the straw. "Andis." It was the first word he could speak.

She frowned. "Locke killed him, then collapsed. I called the ambulance, and they brought you and Locke here. He's down the hall. They're talking about surgery, because he's bleeding in his brain."

Conner hated that he was responsible for all of this. Locke wouldn't be here if Conner had done his job and kept Kayla out of this. Though if anyone was tough enough to survive something like that, it was the director. Conner needed to call Greg, tell him what had happened. Or did he know? Was he here?

Conner squeezed his eyes shut for a second and tried to blink out the thoughts swirling in his head. "I'm sorry." She'd been left alone with the two of them injured and a dead man. She must have been so scared.

Kayla shook her head. "Why on earth would you be sorry?" She quit shaking her head and touched her temple. "Ouch. You saved my life, Conner. I get it. I get why you'd do that, because I wanted to do that for you."

She thought he'd let her die? That he'd have allowed her to do what he'd done. Conner's breath came in a rush, machines started to beep loudly and a nurse rushed in.

"You need to relax, Mr. Thorne." The nurse touched his shoulder. "I'll go tell the doctor you're awake."

When the nurse left, Kayla said, "Okay, that was the wrong thing to say." She set both hands on his shoulders. "I'm okay, Conner. Promise me you'll relax. Otherwise you're going to hurt yourself."

He tried to take a breath, but it was Kayla's hands on his shoulders, his face, that brought his heart rate back to normal.

"That's good. Everything is fine. Locke will be fine, Andis is dead and I'm here. With you." She touched her slender fingers to his cheeks.

Conner turned his head so his lips met her fingers.

She smiled, so sweet. "You don't mind?"

He frowned, not willing to mess this up by

saying the wrong thing. She was offering him everything and he didn't want to ruin it. Or maybe that was just wishful thinking. Maybe she was only here because he'd been shot.

"Okay, now you're overthinking things." Kayla leaned down and touched her smile to his lips. He felt the warmth of her breath on his face. She'd waited here for him and had news about Locke for when he woke. Andis had been killed. She was safe, and he'd saved her.

Thank You, God, that this all worked out. Thank You for giving Kayla to me.

When she pulled back, he cleared his throat. "Kayla."

"Yeah?"

"I love you." He didn't care if she never said it back. If he'd only dreamed it because he'd been hit on the head, plus wishful thinking...

She grinned. "That's good. Because I love you, as well. I always have, Conner. Since that first day in the White House." Her grin turned into a small chuckle. "We fought it—boy, did we fight it. But I think maybe God brought us back together because it's time to stop fighting and admit there's something between us. I needed you, and God gave you back to me."

She straightened, and the smile dropped from her face as though she'd realized what she'd said and wanted to take it back. "This really isn't the time." Before she could back up out of reach, Conner grabbed her arm. Kayla shook her head. "You're hurt. I shouldn't be talking to you about this. Not right now. We can do it later."

He pulled on her arm until she got the message and moved closer to him. "Marry me."

Her lips curled into a smile, and she laughed as she put both hands onto her cheeks. "You think my small-town life, my little church and office hours would suit you? Or am I going to uproot my life and go wherever you end up?" She paused. "You're an undercover agent, Conner. Don't you have to go back to Washington and debrief from this assignment? Then they'll give you a new assignment. There's a lot to work out before we can even think about *marriage*."

She said that, but there was a gleam in her eyes Conner wanted to believe was hope. The same hope he felt when he saw her. Conner said, "You love me."

"Yes."

"I love you. For always, forever. The rest is just details to work out. Okay?"

She chuckled once more. "I'd love to think that. *Just details*. Like Italian or Chinese food?"

"I am hungry."

She shook her head, but she was smiling. "More like putting two lives together. Trying to make this work will be hard. We don't even know if it's possible."

"It'll work."

"How can you be so sure?"

Conner put everything he was feeling into another kiss. When he pulled back, a dreamy look had settled into Kayla's eyes. She looked away, her cheeks flushed. "Because I'm sure. Okay?"

She nodded. Conner kissed her once more, just a small touch of the lips.

The doctor cleared his throat. "It's nice to see you're awake and feeling better."

Conner took Kayla's hand. "I'm feeling a lot better."

EPILOGUE

Six Weeks Later

Kayla saved the file and sat back in the new chair that her father had bought her to replace the one that had been destroyed. She'd spent two weeks at his house, and made sure he was well enough that she didn't feel guilty leaving him again. It hadn't worked.

Her job simply didn't hold the allure it had. Not that she wanted to go chasing thugs again. She had no intention of getting wrapped up in something dangerous. Not ever. The thing that didn't fit, the part that wasn't right—okay, it was just plain *missing*—was the fact that Conner hadn't even called.

Not once since he'd checked out of the hospital and gone back to Washington.

She'd broken down and called him, but he hadn't answered and she didn't want to leave a desperate voice mail that would only make her sound pathetic.

Locke had answered. He was back at work, and he'd told her Conner was busy debriefing. But he had to be finished now. There was no way it took this long. He'd probably gone on to his next assignment. Maybe he had a "forever love" on every job. Maybe she was just—

"Knock, knock."

She whirled around in the chair. "Conner."

He strode in wearing jeans and a T-shirt. And a jacket nothing like that beat-up leather one he'd worn the first time he walked in this office. He looked really, really good.

Especially when his lips curved up like that. "You're blushing."

Kayla cleared her throat and stood. "I guess I'm just…surprised to see you, is all."

"That's valid." He closed the door and walked to her.

"How are you?"

He touched the spot on his chest where the shot had hit him. "No hole. Still hurts, though. The doctor said it will for a while. No sudden movements, no exertion that will put stress on my body. So here I am. Not even thirty-five and retired."

"That's not the end of the world." Was it the

reason he'd taken so long to come? "There are plenty of things you can do instead."

"Like run for the sheriff of a small town? One like Samson, Virginia?"

Did he...

Conner held out his hands and she set hers in them. "I've done the people of this town wrong. Maybe, if they trust me enough to let me tell them the truth of who I am, they might give me the chance to make it up to them by being their sheriff. It's a long shot, and if I don't make it, then I could get a PI license or find another job."

"I'm sure they'll elect you."

"Yeah?"

"Yes, because I'm going to tell everyone in town what a great sheriff you're going to be." She sucked in a breath and smiled. "Say hi to your campaign manager."

Conner chuckled. "Hi."

"We can get started brainstorming right now."

"So long as we make the time for other things that don't involve talking."

Kayla didn't know what to say. She didn't want to let her heart hope too much, but she had enjoyed every single kiss they'd shared. Was that part of why he was here—and planning to stay, from the sound of it?

Conner pulled a box from his jacket pocket.

A velvet box. "Just so you know—" he held it up "—this is where we're headed. It's going to stay in my pocket until you're ready, until you feel it's the right time to say—"

"Yes."

"Exactly. I want to wait until you think it's the right time."

"No, I mean *yes*. Conner, I don't want to wait. Not if you're sure."

He stared at her silently for a moment. "You're sure?"

"Of course I am. You're here, aren't you? God brought us together for a reason. We helped each other through everything that happened with Andis. Now I know, I'm *certain*, that we can weather anything life throws at us. So long as we do it together."

His brows scrunched together. "That was pretty much exactly the same speech I was going to give you."

"Uh…sorry."

"It sounded better coming from you."

Kayla smiled. "Thanks."

Conner opened the box and held it up. A diamond on a setting of gorgeous stones. Blessings upon blessings. "You're sure?"

Kayla nodded. "I'm so sure."

He took the ring from the box. "Will you marry me?"

Conner slid the ring on her finger.

"Forever. For always. Yes."

* * * * *

If you enjoyed SECURITY DETAIL,
look for these other great books from
author Lisa Phillips,
available now.

DOUBLE AGENT
STAR WITNESS
MANHUNT
EASY PREY
SUDDEN RECALL
DEAD END

Find more great reads at
www.LoveInspired.com

Dear Reader,

I'm so glad you've embarked with me on this new series! I'm looking forward to seeing more into the lives of the men and women who are Secret Service agents.

Conner and Kayla had a history, one that was at times a joy and at times a pain to delve into. None of us want to hide our true feelings because circumstances don't allow us to express them, but that is what they had to do. It was wonderful to craft a story where God got the credit for bringing them back together.

I praise and thank Him for the ways He has done that in my life, and my prayer is that He will show you ways He's shown His mighty hand in your life.

If you want to tell me about it, feel free to email lisaphillipsbks@gmail.com. I would love to hear the story. You can also contact me through my website at www.authorlisaphillips.com and sign up for my newsletter while you're there!

May God richly bless you.
Lisa Phillips

Get 2 Free Books,
Plus 2 Free Gifts—
just for trying the Reader Service!

Love Inspired®

YES! Please send me 2 FREE Love Inspired® Romance novels and my 2 FREE mystery gifts (gifts are worth about $10 retail). After receiving them, if I don't wish to receive any more books, I can return the shipping statement marked "cancel." If I don't cancel, I will receive 6 brand-new novels every month and be billed just $5.24 for the regular-print edition or $5.74 each for the larger-print edition in the U.S., or $5.74 each for the regular-print edition or $6.24 each for the larger-print edition in Canada. That's a saving of at least 13% off the cover price. It's quite a bargain! Shipping and handling is just 50¢ per book in the U.S. and 75¢ per book in Canada.* I understand that accepting the 2 free books and gifts places me under no obligation to buy anything. I can always return a shipment and cancel at any time. Even if I never buy another book, the 2 free books and gifts are mine to keep forever.

Please check one:

☐ Love Inspired Romance Regular-Print
  (105/305 IDN GLQC)

☐ Love Inspired Romance Larger-Print
  (122/322 IDN GLQD)

Name   (PLEASE PRINT)

Address   Apt. #

City   State/Province   Zip/Postal Code

Signature (if under 18, a parent or guardian must sign)

Mail to the **Reader Service:**
IN U.S.A.: P.O. Box 1867, Buffalo, NY 14240-1867
IN CANADA: P.O. Box 611, Fort Erie, Ontario L2A 9Z9

Want to try two free books from another line?
Call 1-800-873-8635 today or visit www.ReaderService.com.

*Terms and prices subject to change without notice. Prices do not include applicable taxes. Sales tax applicable in N.Y. Canadian residents will be charged applicable taxes. Offer not valid in Quebec. This offer is limited to one order per household. Books received may not be as shown. Not valid for current subscribers to Love Inspired Romance books. All orders subject to credit approval. Credit or debit balances in a customer's account(s) may be offset by any other outstanding balance owed by or to the customer. Please allow 4 to 6 weeks for delivery. Offer available while quantities last.

Your Privacy—The Reader Service is committed to protecting your privacy. Our Privacy Policy is available online at www.ReaderService.com or upon request from the Reader Service.

We make a portion of our mailing list available to reputable third parties that offer products we believe may interest you. If you prefer that we not exchange your name with third parties, or if you wish to clarify or modify your communication preferences, please visit us at www.ReaderService.com/consumerchoice or write to us at Reader Service Preference Service, P.O. Box 9062, Buffalo, NY 14240-9062. Include your complete name and address.

LI17R

Get 2 Free Books,
Plus 2 Free Gifts—
just for trying the _Reader Service!_

HARLEQUIN
HEARTWARMING™

**HOMETOWN HEARTS** ♥

YES! Please send me **The Hometown Hearts Collection** in Larger Print. This collection begins with 3 FREE books and 2 FREE gifts in the first shipment. Along with my 3 free books, I'll also get the next 4 books from the Hometown Hearts Collection, in LARGER PRINT, which I may either return and owe nothing, or keep for the low price of $4.99 U.S./ $5.89 CDN each plus $2.99 for shipping and handling per shipment*. If I decide to continue, about once a month for 8 months I will get 6 or 7 more books, but will only need to pay for 4. That means 2 or 3 books in every shipment will be FREE! If I decide to keep the entire collection, I'll have paid for only 32 books because 19 books are FREE! I understand that accepting the 3 free books and gifts places me under no obligation to buy anything. I can always return a shipment and cancel at any time. My free books and gifts are mine to keep no matter what I decide.

262 HCN 3432 462 HCN 3432

Name _____ (PLEASE PRINT)

Address _____ Apt. #

City _____ State/Prov. _____ Zip/Postal Code

Signature (if under 18, a parent or guardian must sign)

Mail to the **Reader Service:**

IN U.S.A.: P.O. Box 1867, Buffalo, NY. 14240-1867
IN CANADA: P.O. Box 609, Fort Erie, Ontario L2A 5X3

* Terms and prices subject to change without notice. Prices do not include applicable taxes. Sales tax applicable in NY. Canadian residents will be charged applicable taxes. This offer is limited to one order per household. All orders subject to approval. Credit or debit balances in a customer's account(s) may be offset by any other outstanding balance owed by or to the customer. Please allow 4 to 6 weeks for delivery. Offer available while quantities last. Offer not available to Quebec residents.

Get 2 Free Books,
Plus 2 Free Gifts—
just for trying the
Reader Service!